TAKEN BY THE ALIEN WARRIOR

HOPE HART

CHAPTER ONE

E*llie*

UNLIKE MOST PEOPLE, I ALWAYS BELIEVED IN ALIENS. DON'T get me wrong—I never thought they were part of a giant conspiracy, hidden by all the governments on Earth. But I always thought it was supremely arrogant for us humans to believe we were alone in the universe. That our planet just so happened to be the only one capable of supporting intelligent life.

Please.

"Earth to Crazy Pants," a voice sounds, and I ignore it, continuing to rock back and forth.

I was as surprised as anyone when the Arcav made it clear that they were now in charge. But I shrugged my shoulders, did my compulsory blood test, and almost fainted with relief when I wasn't a genetic match and therefore not an Arcav mate.

"Yeah, her lights are on, but no one's home."

I ignore that too, my rocking picking up speed.

I never thought I'd won the genetic lottery until that point. I'd been the last kid picked in gym, I'd never been particularly fast on my feet, and as much as I can appreciate the Arcav's incredible bodies and lethal-looking horns, there's no way I'll ever be strong enough to deal with a male like that.

"She's totally checked out." The first voice sounds irritated. "We need to work together if we have a shot of getting out of here."

I'm a kindergarten teacher. Plus, I have a boyfriend. Kind of. He's a friend, anyway. And a few weeks ago, it looked like he would kiss me. Then he blushed and turned away, mumbling something I couldn't hear. Tim's kind and interesting. Plus, he's dedicated to his job, just like me. Sure, he's kinda geeky, but so am I.

The ship shudders, and I blink. It's getting more and more difficult to pretend I'm not being abducted by aliens. No matter how much I try to wake up, it's just not happening.

Voices sound across the cage. I shake my head. Across the *room*. I can't be in a cage. That's not happening to me.

"Girl, get down. They'll hurt you!" someone shouts.

"Where are we?" a woman asks, and I mentally roll my eyes. Even I can figure that out, and I'm buried so deep in denial I'm almost choking on it.

"I-I think it's some sort of alien ship," someone replies. "We've all been kidnapped. You were one of the last to wake up."

Not me. I was one of the first.

No one speaks as a huge shape blocks the light. I squeeze my eyes closed like a child. If I can't see the alien, maybe it can't see me.

"Sit," the voice rumbles, and my eyes fly open. A fucking Grivath is in the cage with us—a hulking gray monster that looks like he could easily eat us and spit out our bones.

"Where are we?" the same woman asks, and I have to admire her spine. She may be an idiot, but at least she's not pretending she's still at home in her safe bed like I am.

I lift my head enough to see the creature's grin.

"Nowhere near your planet."

A scream leaves her throat, and I sit up, scooting back to the huddle of women who are hugging the wall.

"Let me go home! I need to go home!" she cries. She lunges, attempting to hit him, and he pulls a strange weapon, firing it at her until she falls to the hard floor.

Someone's murmuring to the woman, likely making sure she's all right. I jolt as someone touches my shoulder, and they quickly snatch their hand back as if I'm a wild animal.

I turn and meet huge amber eyes set in a striking face.

"What's your name?" the woman whispers, and I swallow.

"Eleanor—Ellie."

"Ellie, my name is Nevada. It's going to be all right, okay?"

Tears finally fill my eyes. Maybe this is the acceptance part. "You really think so?"

She nods firmly, and I blow out a breath. I wish I had a drop of Nevada's confidence.

I don't know how much time passes, but we all sit in silence, scared to draw the attention of the Grivath. His people have been at war with for the Arcav for centuries, but the Arcav promised to keep humans safe.

Major fail, assholes. We're a long way from safety.

When the Grivath returns, it's with a large group of his

huge gray friends. One of them reaches for Nevada, and she scoots back, kicking out at him. He simply grabs her by the arm, and it's as if her punches and kicks don't even register as he hauls her away.

I get to my knees, wishing I could do something, anything, but then I'm shrieking as a Grivath reaches for me, throwing me over his shoulder.

My struggles are useless, but I can hear the other women screaming as we're all carried out. I lift my head and see the women who are left staring after us, shocked.

Do something! I want to scream at them, but they're stuck in a cage. There's nothing they can do.

The Grivath carries me down a long corridor, following the screams of the other women taken from the cage.

Eventually, the air becomes warmer, and I bounce on the Grivath's shoulder as he walks down some stairs. Sounds assault my ears. After the tense quiet of the cage, it's terrifying, and thanks to the translator in my ear, I can make out some of the words roared in the distance.

When I was young, my dad flipped houses. He'd take me to auctions, and I loved the excitement of the crowd almost as much as I loved spending time with my dad. The auctioneer confused me, but dad would simply laugh and lift me onto his shoulders when he decided not to bid anymore so I could watch and listen.

That's exactly what this is. Some of my most cherished memories have been replaced with this nightmare.

We're suddenly surrounded by aliens as the Grivath walk us through the crowd. No one dares touch, but they discuss us as if we're cattle at a market.

"Human females," someone mutters. "Expensive but worth it."

Dear God, please tell me I'm not going to be sold at an auction.

The world spins, and I'm suddenly placed on my feet. I stumble as the blood rushes from my head, and sniggers sound from the crowd.

I'm standing on a long, raised platform with all the other women. One by one, aliens from the crowd bid on us, the winners taking their women as soon as their auctions are finished, ignoring their desperate screams.

I try to tune it all out. In my mind, the avid gazes staring at us are really my kindergarteners looking up at me from their desks. My denial almost works until it's my turn.

I don't understand what the shouted numbers mean, but I stand on the platform in my flannel pajamas and stare over the crowd. The auctioneer is a tall greenish alien with a tail, and he uses that tail to poke my hip, making the crowd roar with amusement as I shriek and slap it away.

This seems to drive up my price, and I turn my head, meeting Nevada's gaze. She's standing with another group of women who seem to have been bought together. It doesn't escape me that they're all gorgeous. Nevada's tall, curved in all the right places, and her toned, tan legs speak of an active lifestyle. She's obviously fit, and muscles dance in her arm when she attempts to shrug off the purple alien holding her.

The bidding continues, and I let my mind wander, choosing not to be here while I'm sold like a piece of meat. Why were we taken? How were we chosen? I run my gaze over the other human women, all of whom look like they could model professionally. I'm the odd one out, and my brain immediately goes to work, attempting to figure out how this could have happened.

I'm practically estranged from my mother, but I was in

Louisiana on a rare visit to her and my sister when I was taken.

Amelia.

Ah, it all makes sense now. I bet the Grivath took me by mistake. One more thing to blame my sister for.

I can no longer ignore the roars of the crowd, and even my ability to mentally go elsewhere fails as one of the purple aliens grins, pleased. He's obviously the winner, and I'm pushed along until I reach Nevada and the other women.

Two more women are sold into our group. One of them trips, falling to her knees as she sobs too hard to watch where she's going. A purple alien immediately kicks her, and we all hear a crack as his foot hits her ribs.

One of his friends snaps at him, dragging the woman to her feet and pushing her toward us.

"Are you okay?" I murmur, and she simply shakes her head, bent over as she gasps for air.

There are still more women left on the stage, but the assholes who bought our group gesture for us to move.

We all ignore them until one of them reaches for a weapon similar to the one that the Grivath used on the screaming woman back on the other ship.

Just like that, we're all moving. No one wants to experience the complete incapacitation that comes from a shock like that.

I study the aliens as we're marched back toward where we came from. It's some kind of dock, with a row of ships parked next to the one the Grivath used.

The aliens are a pale purple color, with curved horns that remind me of goats. They're vicious, quick to hit and kick if we don't move quickly enough. The alien behind me gets impatient when I hesitate and jolts me with the weapon in his hand.

I scream, pain hitting my entire body. But the weapon is obviously not as bad as the one the Grivath used because I manage to stay on my feet, terrified of falling to the ground where I'd be even more vulnerable.

Finally, we stop, and the aliens gesture for us to climb the stairs to their ship.

We all glance at each other as we take in our new ride. It looks like a rust bucket. If it were a car, it certainly wouldn't be roadworthy.

"Move!" one of the aliens screams at us, waving his weapon threateningly, and we all jump into motion, climbing the stairs.

It can't have been an hour since we were brought here, and we've already been sold. Terror hits me, and my knees are shaking almost too badly for me to walk up the stairs.

Our lives will never be the same.

Terex

Rakiz eyes me over the fire, and I stare back. My king respects strength and quickly grows tired of those who scrape and kneel.

Today, though, his mood is dark.

"One of our mishua was taken last night. From right under our noses. The Voildi are becoming bolder."

I grit my teeth. The Voildi have been a problem for centuries. If we had the forces, we could kill them all, making this planet a safer place for everyone.

Unfortunately, unlike us, they do not suffer from a

shortage of females. They continue to breed and breed, and now they come to our territory and dare to take a mishua?

"They must be taught a lesson," I say.

Rakiz shifts, finally gesturing to a servant, who offers me a drink. I reach out for the offered cup, enjoying the burn as the cool noptri removes some of the tension from my shoulders.

I wait for Rakiz to speak. This is where we usually disagree. I may be in charge of our forces, but I am a warrior first. His attempts to keep me from hunting have long caused tension between us.

Ultimately, I will obey my king's orders for the good of our tribe. But I don't have to like them.

Rakiz narrows his eyes as if reading my mind, and I raise an eyebrow, shifting my weight. After a long day of training with my men, I would prefer to find a willing female to tumble beneath me and then sleep the night away. I frown. Recently, the tumble has not been worth the inevitable tears and tantrums that follow when the female in question realizes that I do not have any plans to take a mate.

Perhaps just a hot meal and a good sleep, then.

"Send Deraz and Asroz," he says.

I grit my teeth. "Respectfully, the Voildi must feel that they have enough numbers to take anyone we send if they are brave enough to come so far into our territory. Deraz and Asroz will need help. They are not yet seasoned enough to take down an entire pack of Voildi."

Rakiz stares at me. "And I suppose they need my most experienced warrior to go with them."

"Actually—"

"Enough."

I grind my teeth, heeding Rakiz's warning tone. But my eyes likely show my displeasure because he finally sighs.

"With our forces in the North, we are coming perilously close to having too few warriors here to protect the tribe from attack. You have three days to remove this pack of Voildi from the face of this planet."

I nod. The Voildi stink, and they are terrible at concealing their tracks. Three days is longer than I had expected.

"Thank you," I say, getting up to leave.

Rakiz sighs. "Be careful."

I nod again and exit his tashiv, inhaling the brisk air. Winter is finally making way for warmer weather, but the nights are still cold, and I shrug my cloak over my shoulders, taking a moment to run a finger over the long cut in the material.

"That needs to be repaired," a voice says, and I turn.

Learza smiles at me.

"I must leave tomorrow on a hunt," I say, and her face falls. "I will have it fixed when I return."

She nods, her eyes meeting mine. "I would be happy to stay with you tonight," she says boldly.

I eye her. I tumbled Learza many years ago. I would never tell her, but it was a mistake. I had assumed it was two friends releasing some tension. She thought it was a guarantee that she would be the last female in my bed.

With so few females available, they have many warriors to choose from. However, many of them wish for a life closer to the throne.

Rakiz has no heir and no brothers, which means that I remain next in line should he fall. But I will lay down my own life before I allow that to happen. I have never met a better, more just ruler than our king.

I am already forced to spend too much time close to our camp and not enough time hunting and fighting. I would wither away if I were forced to make decisions over others' lives and prevented from hunting the Voildi.

"Thank you," I say. "But I must rest before we leave at dawn."

***

Ellie

New ship, new cage. These aliens don't seem to care if we talk, and they've left us alone after dumping us in a cage even smaller than the one on the last ship.

A woman is currently pacing back and forth in front of the locked cage door. Other than me, she's the shortest woman here, but where I'm curvy and plump, she's tiny and petite, so I've mentally nicknamed her Tinker Bell.

"We have to get out of here," she hisses, and Nevada nods her head.

"How though? Those bastards have the keys."

"What's the end goal?" another voice speaks up, and I turn to the woman who was kicked in the ribs when she fell. Her face is still pale as she sits hunched over and leaning against the wall.

"What do you mean?" Nevada asks.

"Well, say we get out of here. You think we can kill those aliens and take this ship? Any of you guys flown a spaceship before?"

Her tone is lightly sarcastic, but she's not wrong.

"What do you think, Ellie?" Nevada asks.

I hesitate. There are more of us than there are of them, unless they had a bunch of aliens staying put on the ship while their friends bought us. But this is a pretty small ship. The problem? They're armed.

I chew my lip and shrug. "The weapons are an issue."

Another woman snorts. "That's putting it lightly."

Of all of us, this woman is the one who stands out. She was wearing red lingerie when she was taken, and she has the body of a Victoria's Secret model. She stood on that stage as if she was bored, rolling her eyes while she was auctioned.

Lingerie's face was pale, and her hands shook, but you have to admire someone who can bullshit their way through life with that kind of confidence.

Another woman shifts, raising her hand, and blushes at Lingerie's snort. Tinker Bell sends Lingerie a look and nods at the hand raiser.

She shivers in her thin T-shirt, and I finger my flannel. I've never been happier to sleep in completely unsexy flannel pajamas. While I'm cold, I'm not shivering as much as some of the other women.

"Do any of you have any kind of training?" Hand-Raiser asks. "Do you think we could take them down?"

Nevada nods. "I'm a marine. I'm willing to give it a try."

I raise my eyebrows. That explains the muscles and the attitude. For the first time, I feel a spark of hope.

"Anyone else?" I ask.

"I'm a firefighter with a black belt in karate," one of the women says, and Nevada smiles.

"Excellent." Nevada glances at the rest of us, and we all shake our heads. There are eight of us, and only two have any experience with combat.

I sigh. For a split second, I got my hopes up. My talents lie elsewhere. I can comfort a crying six-year-old or convince a child that putting their pencil up their nose isn't a good idea, but I'm not tough or strong. And the thought of taking on one of those aliens...

But what other choice do we have? Wherever they're taking us next is guaranteed to be even worse than where we are now. The kind of people who buy other people aren't likely to treat us well. We could end up anywhere, and I bet the Arcav don't even know we've been taken yet.

"Okay," Tinker Bell says. "Let's see how many of them they send in here at once. If it's just one, maybe we can all attack if they open the cage door."

We all nod, and determination hits me. We're not going down without a fight.

The ship shudders, and I grab onto the bars of our cage as it jolts and lurches.

"What the fuck's happening now?" Hand-Raiser shrieks.

The shuddering suddenly stops, and we're all panting and pale as we look at each other, wide-eyed.

What's worse than being abducted and trapped on an alien spaceship? Being abducted and trapped on an alien spaceship that looks like it's seen better days. If this ship falls apart, we're instantly dead.

"What did I do to end up here? What could I have done differently?"

Nevada sends me a sympathetic look, and I realize I'm mumbling aloud.

"Sometimes," she says, "we do everything right, and life just plain sucks anyway."

We try to get a few hours' sleep, shivering and huddling together. There's not much else to say. All of us are freezing and starving, and our alien captors don't seem too concerned about giving us food or water.

Maybe that means that we'll soon be wherever they're taking us.

That's not necessarily a good thing. But I'm so thirsty that when I manage to briefly fall asleep, I dream of streams and ponds, rivers and oceans. I almost cry when I wake up with a dry mouth and chapped lips. We're all so dehydrated that none of us have needed to use the bucket in the corner of our cage yet.

A shriek leaves my throat as the ship shudders again. This time, it's jolting from side to side violently, and I see stars as my head cracks against the bars of our cage. The woman who was kicked in the ribs screams in pain as she flies across the cage, hitting the wall.

An alarm begins to wail, a red light flashing as we all cover our ears at the piercing sound. I wish there was a window in here so I could see outside. Then again, if we're all about to die, maybe it's better not to know.

We're left completely alone. None of the purple aliens come to check on us, but I can hear footsteps thumping above us. We cling together, a group of women who were strangers yesterday but may die together today.

The shrieking gets louder, and I huddle lower, pressing my hands harder against my ears as screams sound over the alarm.

And then everything goes black.

CHAPTER TWO

E*llie*

I cough, my mouth a desert as I suck in air, choking on smoke. I'm trapped under something warm.

Someone warm. I crack my eyes open and manage to roll the firefighter off me, relief hitting me at her groan. At least one other woman is alive.

I sit up, hissing as I put pressure on my elbow. It's either sprained or broken, and I cradle it as I take in our cage.

Tinker Bell's lying against the back wall, not moving, her head covered in blood. Nevada is crouched over her, holding a piece of what used to be a T-shirt to her head.

I lean over and shake the firefighter, who opens her eyes, groaning again as she does so.

"Everyone alive?" Nevada asks.

A woman who introduced herself as Beth hisses as she sits up, clutching her side, and the firefighter groans again.

"Fuck," she says. "This is the girls' trip from hell."

I snort at that, and suddenly we're all laughing, most of us hysterically. I wipe away tears of laughter as Tinker Bell finally sits up, and we all stare at each other in shock.

Our situation has gone from bad to worse.

I hear no movement above us, but our cage door is still locked. Unless we can get it open, we're destined to starve to death in here.

It's a bad way to go.

We all freeze as something moves above us, and then we're once again huddled together like frightened sheep. We're all silent as we eye the stairs, listening as someone walks down them.

It's a species of alien I've never seen before. And he looks as surprised to see us as we are to see him.

He's about Lingerie's height, with pale yellow skin similar to my grandmother's when she had jaundice. He smiles at us, and I shudder at his teeth. They remind me of my roommate's cat's, perfectly ready to puncture the skin of his prey.

He calls up the stairs, and more of his friends appear, all wearing thin loincloths and not much else. His friends seem as shocked as him, but they instantly smile at us as he moves forward.

"My name is Karok," he says. "We will find the key to your cage and take you back to our tribe for food and medical care."

We all blow out sighs of relief, and he grins at us as he gestures at one of the other aliens, who nods and clomps his way back upstairs.

"How did you get here?"

Beth sniffs. "We were stolen from our beds and sold on a strange planet. Where are we now?"

Karok's mouth drops open, his eyes wide. I guess you don't hear stories like that every day.

"This planet is called Agron," he says as his friend returns, holding a key. I almost cry in relief as he pushes it into the lock and the cage door swings open.

We file out of the cage, and Tinker Bell snarls at one of the aliens who can't seem to keep his eyes off the blood pouring from her head. She needs a doctor.

We're all hurt, my elbow sending blinding pain up my arm each time I move it. But head injuries are the worst, and they're the most likely to kill you.

We slowly make our way upstairs, and my mouth drops open. The aliens are dead, and not all of them from the crash. I eye Karok, who smiles at me again. I'm not an idiot. I watch *CSI*. And there has been one hell of a fight up here.

Lingerie growls at me to keep walking, and I take two steps out of the ship only to freeze, ignoring her curse as she slams into me.

I can see the sky. The green sky.

Oh God. It really happened. We're really on an alien planet. The sky isn't a dark green, more of a turquoise, but it's nothing I've ever seen on Earth.

"Well, at least we can breathe the air," Nevada says, and my throat almost closes in panic at the thought of not being able to.

The aliens help us climb down from the wreckage until we're all standing in front of the ship.

"If you will follow us," Karok says, "we will be back at our camp by nightfall.

I grew up in the South, where a simple "bless your heart" can mean everything from "you're an idiot" to "fuck you." From the time I was a small child, my sister and mother would smile even as they hissed hurtful words and backhanded compliments. I quickly learned not to trust what people say.

Trust what they do instead.

These new aliens are all smiles, showcasing their sharp teeth. They haven't touched us, other than to help us from the ship, but something about the way their eyes dart between us and the way they murmur to each other has the hair on the back of my neck standing up.

"Are you sure we should trust them?" I mutter to Nevada.

She raises her eyebrow in surprise, but it's Lingerie who speaks up.

"Who else do you see around here helping us escape that awful ship? They promised us food, water, and doctors. What more do you want?"

The others are silent, no one jumping to my defense, and I shrug. Lingerie sends me an impatient look and turns, beaming at Karok. "We're ready when you are."

Firefighter moves closer to me. She's a redhead, she looks strong and fit, and she's wearing Mickey Mouse pajamas. "Don't worry, girl. We're survivors. These aliens try anything, and we'll make them beg for mercy."

I like her attitude, but she's greatly overestimating my ability to make anyone beg for anything.

"What's your name?"

She smiles at me. "Ivy. You're Ellie, right?"

We talk for a few minutes, but we're mostly too stunned to pay attention to each other.

We've been walking for hours when I contemplate sitting down and just not getting back up. Everything hurts. Tinker Bell's head won't stop bleeding, so we manage to tear most of one leg off my flannel pajama pants to use as a rough bandage. Ivy helps me make a sling for my arm with the other leg of my pajamas, and we're a quiet group as we follow Karok and his friends.

The forest is just plain creepy. The huge trees have white trunks, the branches reaching toward us like bony fingers. We're all jumpy, tensing at every sound even as we peer into the dark forest, keeping an eye out for beasties.

There are ten or twelve of the new aliens, but other than Karok, none of them introduce themselves to us. They mostly just talk amongst themselves in hushed voices. Within a couple of hours, my thighs are burning—both from the difficult terrain and the chafing as they rub together.

Tears prick my eyes, and I regret all the times I complained about my life in New York. If I had known that this is how I'd end up, abducted on an alien planet, my thighs rubbing together so much they're practically starting a fire, I would've appreciated my quiet life.

"I need a break," Tinker Bell finally says quietly. I glance at her, and my mouth drops open. I know head wounds bleed more than almost any other injury, but she looks like a zombie—bruised, so pale she's almost gray, and covered in blood.

I wince as I step on a particularly sharp stone. None of us have shoes, and our feet are paying the price.

Karok frowns. "We must keep moving if we are to make it to our camp by nightfall."

Nevada narrows her eyes at him. "Charlie isn't feeling well. We can take ten minutes."

Charlie. At least I can stop calling her Tinker Bell now. We all stop in solidarity, all of us needing a break. My mouth is so dry I'm attempting to collect my spit, and I glance at where Karok is huddled with two other aliens.

"Please," I say, my voice hoarse. "Do you know where we can find some water?"

Karok smiles at us again, and I can't explain why, but I see my death in that smile. He shakes his head, and I scowl at him.

We're standing in a small clearing, surrounded by trees. Surely there has to be a lake or a river—or even a fucking pond—somewhere, right?

I glance around, planning my exit route, which is why I'm the first to see the warriors when they appear.

Terex

We have managed to track the Voildi to an area just beyond our territory. From the stink they left behind, they have once again crossed through our domain. They grow ever bolder.

I hear voices in a language I have not heard before. Thankfully, when our planet was discovered by visitors centuries ago, they carried translator chips, which are inserted deep within the ear canal. These chips allow all species on Agron to understand each other.

We all freeze, stunned as a voice sounds.

A female.

Another replies, her voice musical and soft, and something in my gut clenches. I must know the owner of that voice.

I glance at Deraz and Asroz, and they nod, moving to surround the Voildi. I don't understand how they found these females and why the females are not screaming and crying at the thought of being taken by the Voildi.

I move closer and look through the trees, careful to stay

out of sight. There are more than two females; in fact, I count eight at first glance. One of them is bleeding heavily and surrounded by three females. I nod, approving. We must ensure that they are kept together so that they will not be killed by the Voildi when we attack.

"Please," a female says, and the rest of the world falls away as I watch her. This was the voice I heard earlier. "Do you know where we can find some water?"

I almost snort as one of the Voildi smiles at her and shakes his head. The Voildi could not care less if their prey is dying of thirst.

The female doesn't look pleased at this response and narrows her eyes at him, glancing around as if she is considering leaving to find water herself.

She is small and shapely, her skin pale, although her cheeks are flushed. I scan her body, frowning. She holds her arm to her as if it pains her, and like the other females, she is covered in bruises.

Her hair is light and falls down her back to her waist, knotted and tangled. I find myself wishing I could brush that glorious hair while she relaxes by my fire, and my gaze is immediately drawn to her plump ass and full breasts.

This female looks as if she was made to be tumbled.

Her shoulders slump as she glances at the other females, and I watch the exact moment she decides not to leave them.

I want to roar with rage. If we had not managed to track the Voildi, that decision would have cost the tiny female her life.

I force myself to look elsewhere, finding Asroz and Deraz in position. I signal to them, and they nod. The Voildi have become overconfident. If they were not so eager to get their prey back to their camp, they would have spread out around the clearing, guarding the females.

Their mistake.

We lunge into the clearing as one, roaring. The females begin screaming, jumping away from us—most of them moving further from the Voildi.

I meet the terrified eyes of the female with the incredible voice and growl at her fear. She was following the Voildi to certain death, and yet she bares her teeth at me and moves to protect the other females?

I force my attention away and draw my sword.

We're immediately surrounded, and I laugh as the thrill of the battle hits me and the Voildi pull knives and smaller swords. While the Voildi are much smaller than us, they travel in larger packs, often falling on our warriors like rabid wolves. Their smaller size makes them fast, but they are no match for us this day.

I slash my sword and hear retching from the females as one of the Voildi's heads falls to the ground. The next is not so quick to step into my path, but he falls just as quickly as the first.

"Help!"

Screams sound, and I turn, dodging a strike from a Voildi who has managed to sneak up behind me. The females are still separated, and more Voildi have appeared, taking advantage of the battle to take the females and run.

These Voildi are from another pack, with their skin a darker shade of yellow and an unusual style of dress—long pants and shirts instead of the more typical loincloths.

The Voildi we are fighting become incensed, growling at them even as we cut them down. The other pack of Voildi grin, each lifting a struggling female as they disappear through the trees.

Asroz snarls, attempting to go after them, but he's surrounded, our enemies endeavoring to take his head.

The other females fight to get to their friends, but it would be suicide to to cross the area where we are fighting the Voildi.

Deraz roars, kicking out at a Voildi, driving him close to me where I slide my sword between his ribs before pulling it out as he slumps to his knees and beheading him in one stroke.

More retching from behind us.

Who are these females with their soft stomachs? Braxian females are used to seeing the realities of battle.

I grit my teeth as Deraz attempts to follow the stolen females, narrowly missing a knife to the gut.

"Focus," I order him. "You are no use to the females if you're dead."

It takes time to dispatch the rest of the Voildi. Time we don't have. Finally, though, all of them are dead, and I check on Deraz and Asroz before meeting the eyes of the tiny, light-haired female. She holds my gaze steadily before her eyes dart away to Deraz and Asroz as they move closer. I growl, needing her attention, and her eyes jump to mine again, even as an indignant voice sounds.

"Who the fuck are you guys, and why did you kill our rescuers?"

CHAPTER THREE

E *llie*

"My name is Terex, and this is Deraz and Asroz," the giant alien growls. He's huge, and his muscles flex as he takes a step forward. His hair falls to his shoulders, pulled away from his face in small plaits decorated with beads and pieces of leather. His shirt is ripped, and I can see what look like blue scales down one side of his shoulder.

In short, he's both incredibly sexy and completely terrifying.

"You think they're overcompensating with those swords?" Hand-Raiser murmurs, and Nevada snorts.

"*We* are your rescuers," he says. "Those creatures are Voildi, and they would have taken you back to their camp, slaughtered you, and eaten you over the next few days."

I feel the blood drain from my face.

"No wonder Ellie was so popular," Lingerie says. "She'd be a meal and a half."

"What the fuck, Vivian?" Nevada snaps.

I blush, turning away as I feel Terex's eyes on me. All it takes is one insult, and I'm eleven years old again, listening to my mother bemoan the fact that I can't fit into Amelia's old pageant dresses.

I blow out a breath. *Vivian*, huh? We all deal with trauma in different ways, and maybe Vivian deals with hers by being a giant bitch.

"I *told* you guys there was something weird about them," I mutter.

Vivian turns from where she was checking out the aliens and narrows her eyes at me. "Then why didn't you grow a spine and fight harder?"

"Enough, Vivian," Nevada says. "You were the one who shot her down when she said she didn't trust them."

Vivian opens her mouth but snaps it shut as Nevada's eyes narrow at her.

Nevada turns to Terex. "Some of those Voildi took Beth, Zoey, and Ivy," she says. "We have to find them."

Terex exchanges glances with the other warriors while I scan the clearing. "You guys. Charlie isn't here either. Did you see who took her?"

Blank faces. Shit.

"At the very least, she had a concussion. We need to see if she wandered off somewhere," I say firmly. "Maybe she decided to hide."

Thankfully, everyone agrees with me, and we begin checking the trees beyond the clearing. I search with Hand-Raiser, who tells me her name is Alexis, and we look for places Charlie might have curled up, hoping to hide.

The warriors help, and we call Charlie's name until our voices are hoarse and the warriors shake their heads, herding us back into the clearing.

"We will take you back to our camp, where you can eat and rest," Terex declares.

Alexis snorts. "You know, we've heard that before," she says, and Nevada nods in agreement, her eyes widening at the look on my face.

"You think we should trust him?" Her voice is a murmur, and the warriors pretend to give us a moment to talk, but I have no doubt they can hear every word.

"That huge alien has kind eyes," I say, ignoring Vivian's snort. He *does* have kind eyes. They're a light blue, almost violet, and they're clear and honest. "Plus," I sigh. "We're all hurt and seriously dehydrated. At this point, we have no choice."

"Okay," Nevada says. "I'll stay and look for the other women."

Terex immediately shakes his head. "It's not safe."

She gives him a look, and he stares her down.

"As soon as we get to camp, my king will send more warriors to find them."

Nevada hesitates, and Terex gestures toward Alexis and me. Vivian is scratched and bruised, I'm pretty sure my elbow is broken, and Alexis is limping.

"Your friends need you," he says, and Nevada bites her lip as she glances at us, obviously torn.

"Zoey has broken ribs," she says. "God knows what those assholes will do to the other women."

She's right. Maybe we should all try and find them now.

Asroz strides forward. "Right now, the Voildi have a head start. If we attempt to track them with three injured females, they will simply prepare a trap with the rest of their pack. It is faster and smarter to get back to camp and send experienced hunters who are fresh and well rested."

He's got a point, and Nevada finally nods in agreement.

Terex moves forward. "We will need to walk to where we have tethered our mishua," he says, and I hope to God he's talking about some kind of horse.

We all nod, and I find myself fighting back tears at the thought of more walking.

It's okay, Ellie. Just get through the next bit, and you'll either get to sleep, or you'll be dinner. Either way, this nightmare will be over.

Terex walks close to me as we slowly shuffle out of the clearing and back the way we came. We're in bad shape, too exhausted and stunned to talk. I feel like someone has punched me in the gut at the thought of leaving with the other women missing, but the warriors are right—we're all hurt, and none of us have any experience on this planet.

I'm light-headed and feel like I could puke. I don't know if it's the pain from my elbow or the dehydration, but all I want to do is curl up next to one of these huge, creepy white trees and sleep. Maybe I'll wake up to find that this was all a nightmare.

I stumble over a tree root, and fireworks explode in front of my eyes as the movement jostles my arm. It's weirdly numb and achy if I keep it still, but if I move it, the pain almost drives me to my knees. I can't imagine how much Zoey's hurting right now.

"Female," a deep voice intones, and I turn. Terex gestures for me to turn back around, and I comply, my body tense as he unties and reties my sling. His hands are cool and assured as they brush my neck, and he soon has the sling in a tighter, more supportive position.

"Thank you."

It's a long walk, and I have a lot of time to think. Instead of brooding about the things I can't control, I spend my time wisely— checking out the giant warrior who saved us.

Everything about him speaks of self-assured confidence —from his piercing gaze to his wide shoulders and the way he holds his head high as he scans our surroundings. The two other warriors seem to defer to him, but he still listens to what they have to say. He's obviously tense, and all three of them are on high alert in case more Voildi appear. But he still noticed I was in pain and took the time to attempt to ease it by adjusting my sling.

I catch Vivian running her eyes over his huge body and immediately flick my gaze away. So that's how it'll be.

Finally, we enter another clearing, and all of us women stop in shock as we take in our rides.

"What the hell are they?" Nevada murmurs.

"Our mishua," Deraz says, looking confused. "Have you never seen one before?"

"We're not exactly from around here," I mutter, and Alexis laughs.

The only thing these strange beasts have in common with horses is that they can both be ridden. At least I assume so, since all four of them have some sort of saddles on them. Oh, and just like horses, they have four legs.

But that's where the similarities end. The mishua are dark green, with thick scales covering their bodies and heads that remind me of a lizard or even a dinosaur. Their huge teeth gleam in the sunlight, and their heads are covered in thick horns that rise from their snouts, becoming even bigger as they make their way up to the top of their heads.

"They're dino-horses," Nevada says in a low voice.

I bite my lip. With their red eyes and scaly skin, they look a little like something out of *Jurassic Park*. The thought of getting near them makes me want to turn around and take my chances with the Voildi.

"Don't be afraid, female," Terex says, and I turn to find him studying me. "We will not allow them to hurt you."

"You know, the more comforting thing to say would be, 'They won't hurt you,'" Alexis mutters.

Terex shrugs. Then the warriors all reach into the leather bags attached to their dino-horses and pull out water skins.

They hand them to us, and I almost cry in relief. I take a gulp and then force myself to take small sips, worried that it'll come back up. Once we've handed the water back, Terex gestures for us to step forward.

"We have four mishua, as we were hoping to bring back meat for the tribe. Which of you would feel the most comfortable riding alone? We will keep it tethered to one of our mishua, and you will be perfectly safe."

Unsurprisingly, Nevada volunteers. We all watch as Terex leads her to the beast's head, introducing her.

"This is Leai," he says. "Offer your hand, and we will see if she accepts you."

We all hold our breaths as Nevada gives the mishua a look that clearly says, *Don't fuck with me.* She holds out her hand, and Leai snorts, bumping it with her huge nose.

"She wants you to pet her," Terex says, the ghost of a smile crossing his face. I attempt to ignore the spark of jealousy deep in my chest and frown, turning my attention back to the other mishua.

I've never had such a strong reaction to a man in my life. Sure, I've had crushes, and none of them have ended particularly well. Maybe it's just the way that my brain is processing the shock of everything that has happened to me. It's looking for some distraction to keep me sane.

A hand on my good arm jolts me from my thoughts, and

I realize I'm staring into space. I'm so tired that I almost fell asleep with my eyes open.

I smile at Deraz, and he grins back. He's also incredibly handsome, although he doesn't make me almost trip over myself with nerves the way Terex does. That's a good thing though.

Deraz leads me to his mishua, and I can't help it—I freeze. Nevada's already on her beast, calmly waiting while she strokes Leai's neck.

Asroz is lifting Alexis onto another mishua, and I take a tiny step forward, attempting to find some courage.

"She will ride with me."

I turn and meet Terex's eyes. "Oh, it's okay," I say. "This mishua is fine."

I take another tiny step forward and freeze again as the mishua eyes me. Deraz gives me a look that says I'm crazy for arguing with Terex and gestures for Vivian to step forward instead.

She shoots me a killing look, and I sigh, turning back to Terex.

He watches me out of those odd-colored eyes and points toward his mishua. "Her name is Kini."

I tremble at the thought of getting closer to the mishua. She's even bigger than the others, and she stares at us, her red eyes slightly narrowed as Terex moves up behind me.

"Shh," he says. "Your fear will startle her. Mishua are very sensitive, and if you are afraid, you will make her afraid too. A frightened mishua is a dangerous mishua."

"Okay." I blow out a breath. Terex talks me through it, his huge body behind mine, his voice a rumble in my ear. He leans forward, taking my hand in his and offering it to the mishua. I'm trembling like a leaf, but I allow it, and Kini snorts at me. If I didn't know better, I'd think the dino-horse was mocking me.

She allows me to pet her, and her eyelids slide to half-mast as I stroke her skin. She's scaly, not unlike a lizard, but she's also warm, and she has the weirdest fur along the bottom of her legs—fluffy and lush. Exactly how did these strange creatures evolve?

I squeak as Terex suddenly lifts me like I weigh nothing. Before I can come to terms with my change in height, I'm planted in the saddle, and he swings his body up behind me, wrapping one arm around my waist.

He turns his head and must give a signal to his friends because we begin walking. I clutch at the front of the saddle with my good hand, hopelessly out of my comfort zone. I never even rode horses on Earth, and now I'm riding a dino-horse on...Agron.

I sigh, and Terex leans forward, murmuring in my ear.

"Relax, female. I will not let you fall."

Strangely, that helps. I can't imagine this strong warrior allowing me to topple off his mishua. At the very least, his friends would mock him or something, right?

"Tell me about yourself," he says, and I tense.

"Why?"

"Why not? I have rescued you from certain death, female. Do I not deserve a reward?"

His voice is teasing, and I wish I could see his face.

"Um. I'm a kindergarten teacher."

"What is this?"

"I teach children."

"Ah, a nurturing female. I can see this."

"What's that supposed to mean?"

"You are gentle and kind. I have only known you for a short time, but I know this."

Gentle and kind. What would it be like to hear him describe me as sexy or hot? A girl can dream.

To be fair, I can't imagine Terex describing anyone as "hot."

Vivian and Deraz ride up next to us, and Deraz and Terex begin talking in low voices. Vivian sends me a look, obviously displeased that I ended up on Terex's dino-horse.

"What are you doing?" she hisses at me, and I stare at her.

"What do you mean?"

"Oh, don't play innocent. You knew I wanted to ride with him."

"I didn't do anything. You're welcome to him, Vivian. I've got more important things to worry about."

The conversation behind us ends, and I stare into the distance. What Vivian doesn't understand is that I'm fully aware of how the universe works. I learned young that the cute, popular guys don't go for shy, nerdy, chubby girls like me. So gorgeous Vivian is welcome to the sexy alien warrior currently clutching me to him, his chin dangerously close to resting on my shoulder.

"What are you thinking?" he murmurs, and I shiver as his breath hits my neck.

"Nothing." I keep my eyes focused ahead, ignoring the frustrated tears that want to rise. I'm just tired. So tired.

When I was fifteen, I had a crush on a football player named Matt. Unlike most of the other football players, he didn't ignore me, never treated me like I was invisible. His locker was next to mine, and occasionally we'd chat about the books we were reading. He was cute, smart, popular, and *nice*.

Within a month, my sister Amelia was dating him. And

she made sure that the rest of my high school years were pure hell.

Women like Amelia and Vivian? Gorgeous women who rule the world with their self-confidence? They get what they want. And the worst thing that someone like me can do is stand in their way.

I wince as I sit deeper in the saddle and the mishua begins going uphill. God, will this day ever end?

"You are hurt," Terex says suddenly, his voice a rumble of displeasure.

"We're all hurt," I mutter.

The chafing is so bad on my thighs that my eyes are hot as I hold back tears. The hours and hours of walking combined with straddling the dino-horse have rubbed the insides of my thighs raw.

I'm not the only one hurting—Alexis is whining too, and I even caught Vivian shifting uncomfortably a few minutes ago. But my thighs are by far the worst. I don't regret ripping off the legs of my pajama pants, but I wish I'd left a little more material behind.

Terex makes a sound, and Kini stops. I turn my head and blink as Terex stares down at me sternly.

"Show me where you're hurt, female."

I scowl at him, suddenly furious. "It's none of your business."

Surprise flashes through his eyes, and then he laughs. My scowl deepens. Glad to know he finds me so funny.

"We'll wait here all day," he declares.

Vivian clears her throat imperiously from where the others are waiting a few feet ahead, and I have a sudden urge to push her off her dino-horse.

I gesture toward my thighs, and Terex frowns and then

growls impatiently. He swings his leg over the mishua, and I jolt as his boots hit the ground. Then he's gently turning me until I'm sitting sidesaddle, gazing down at him.

"You will tell me what is hurting you."

"You're being ridiculous."

He simply stares at me, and I gesture toward my thighs. Terex frowns, and then I'm grabbing at his shoulders as he pushes my thighs further apart, his hands gentle.

"Poor female," he says, his voice low.

I narrow my eyes at him. "My name is Ellie."

He meets my eyes, the expression on his face as if I've given him a gift.

"Poor Ellie." He lingers over my name like it's a dirty word, and I blush. I feel my cheeks heat even more as he returns his attention to my thighs. I'm not the first woman to have chub rub, and I won't be the last. It's just something that happens to plenty of women, especially in summer.

But it's hard being surrounded by perfection, well aware that if I could just lose a few pounds— something that my mother has been hissing at me to do for more than fifteen years— I wouldn't have nearly as much of a problem.

I glance at where the others are waiting. Alexis and Nevada are talking quietly while the guys watch curiously, and Vivian wrinkles her nose at me in disdain.

I want the ground to open up beneath me.

"You're embarrassing me," I hiss at Terex, and to my mortification, a tear spills down my cheek.

Terex's eyes widen, and then his face hardens as he turns to the others, gesturing for them to continue. He waits until they're moving on before he turns back to me.

"Look, I'm fine," I say. "I'll survive until we arrive. Let's just keep going."

"I may not be able to fix your arm, but I can help you with this."

Terex gently runs the tip of one finger over the inside of my thigh, and I wince even as desire stirs in my stomach. I feel my eyes widen, and I glance away, startled.

It's been a long, long time since I've thought about sex, and even longer since I've wanted it. But right now, I'm doing more than thinking about it. I'm visualizing it, fantasizing about it...needing it.

"I have something that will help," Terex says, reaching into one of the leather bags hanging off his saddle.

He pulls out a small jar and opens it. A sweet, floral scent hits me. It's similar and yet different to anything I've ever smelled before.

I reach for the jar, and Terex simply grins up at me, pulling it out of my reach.

His smile... My breath catches, and his grin widens as let out a long sigh. I could've done without seeing that smile. That smile just makes it even harder to ignore what's shaping up to be one hell of a crush.

I'm so busy recovering from the effect his grin has on me that I'm not prepared for his hand to slip between my thighs.

I squeak, pushing at his huge shoulders, and he glowers at me.

"Be still, female," he growls, and I freeze. His touch is matter-of-fact, and it's not like he's attempting to catch a feel, but there's something incredibly intimate about the way his hand strokes the insides of my thighs.

Even though it hurts when he applies the cream, the effect is instant, and I sigh in relief as the pain disappears. Terex studies my face and nods, finally putting the cream away and swinging his leg back over his dino-horse.

"Terex?"

"Yes?"

"Thank you."

CHAPTER FOUR

T*erex*

I FROWN DOWN AT THE FEMALE IN MY ARMS. A FEW HOURS ago, she lost her fight against sleep, and now, exhausted, she slumbers in my arms.

As she should.

These possessive feelings are strange. I do not understand what it is about this female that makes me so drawn to her. Sure, she is beautiful with her lush curves, long hair, and expressive eyes. But she does not seem to trust me at all.

I can tell that she wants me, yet she does not seem to *want* to want me. This is not something I have experienced before, and I long to make her tell me all her secrets.

Ellie has been hurt. It is easy to see by the wounded look in her eyes. I gently ease her closer, and she lets out a tiny, adorable snore. I do not know where these strange females came from, but they are ours now. We will find their friends, and they will join our tribe.

Any tribe that has allowed their females to come to such danger as to be taken by Voildi does not deserve to have them. My king will be pleased at the addition of these new females to our tribe.

Finally, I see our camp in the distance, and Asroz lets out a growl of pleasure. I frown at him as Ellie stirs against me.

"Not a nightmare," she mumbles. "Great."

"We are arriving," I tell her. She nods, but we all remain silent until we reach the outskirts of our camp and are immediately spotted by our sentries.

"Terex?" one of them calls, voice shocked, and I don't blame him. We left to kill Voildi, and we've returned with strange, tiny females.

"Inform the king that I must speak to him," I say, and he nods as he swings open the gate.

While our tribe moves each season, our ongoing fight against the Voildi has meant that we needed to improve our defenses. Now we have more guards surrounding our camp and sentries guarding our mishua night and day.

We ride close to the large pen where the mishua graze and then help the females to find their feet before servants take our mishua to be fed and brushed.

The sentry returns, almost tripping over his feet as he stares, wide-eyed, at the females. "Rakiz is ready for you."

I nod and lead the females across the camp. They are so tired that they can barely walk, and I lean down, murmuring into Ellie's ear. "Would you like me to carry you?"

She glances up at me, and her eyes widen. "Uh, I'm good, thanks."

The females stare silently around the camp. Most families are in their kradis at this time of night, although those who are not are whispering amongst themselves as they watch us walk toward the king's tashiv.

While most of our people have made their homes in large, spacious kradis, Rakiz requires extra space for meetings with his advisors and negotiations with other tribes. His tashiv is warm and welcoming, and I sigh, for once glad to be back in our camp. We walk into the meeting area where Rakiz is waiting, and I hear Ellie inhale sharply as she takes a step closer to me.

There is a reason Rakiz is our king. While he does not fight often, he is still a Braxian warrior that none would challenge.

He scans the group of females, and while no one who does not know him well would see the surprise on his face, I can tell he is shocked by what he sees.

"We found these females traveling with Voildi," I tell him. "They had no idea how much danger they were in."

Rakiz frowns at that. Everyone is aware of the dangers of the Voildi. This is something I also do not understand, and I am interested to hear the females' explanation.

"How is it that you came to be in such a situation?" Rakiz asks.

Unsurprisingly, the female who rode the mishua alone is the one to speak. She seems to be the unofficial leader of the females, and she studies Rakiz in a way that would constitute a challenge if she were a male.

"We were taken from our home planet," she says. "We were then sold on a different planet and loaded into a ship. That ship went down on this planet, and the Voildi appeared. They killed what was left of the aliens who took us and promised us food and water if we went with them."

Rakiz growls and flicks a glance at me. I nod, also stunned. This story does not make any sense. And yet there is no question that these females speak a different language, dress differently, and were willing to trust the

Voildi—something that no female on this planet would ever do.

"We need your help," Nevada continues, and Rakiz returns his attention to her.

"We had other women with us. Three of them were taken by the Voildi in front of us. We don't know what happened to the fourth, but she was seriously injured. We wanted to find them ourselves, but your men assured us that you would send your people to look for them if we came here."

Rakiz studies the female, and I do the same. She does not appear at all discomforted by his silence and simply stares back at him, her spine straight, hands clasped behind her back.

Rakiz nods, his eyes never leaving Nevada. "We will of course help you find your friends. I will send a group of warriors at first light."

Nevada's shoulders slump slightly in relief, and some of the tension eases on her face. "I will go with them."

"You will not."

They stare at each other, the air once again tense and thick.

"Listen," she says softly, "I was taught to leave no man—or woman—behind. I'm going to help find them."

Rakiz gets to his feet, and I sigh. These females are different to any we have known, and my king is studying Nevada as if she is a slightly interesting bug. He lets his eyes move down her body, and she stiffens, tilting her chin higher. Rakiz's eyes stop on one of her knees, which is oozing blood.

He flicks his gaze to me, and I nod. I will ensure all these females are taken directly to the healers.

"We will discuss this in the morning," Rakiz says, and I

raise my brow. It is unlike him to lie. He has made his decision, but he obviously wants the females to eat and rest without arguing.

Nevada nods, and Rakiz turns to one of his servants. "Arana, will you please ensure these females have a chance to bathe, fresh clothes, and food? They will also need somewhere to sleep."

I almost growl at that. My female will be sleeping with me. She just doesn't know it yet.

Ellie

The king is scary. Sure, Terex is scary, but he can also be gentle, with a grin that urges you to grin back. Rakiz simply radiates threat. I don't know how Nevada talked to him the way she did, but I suspect she has a death wish.

When Rakiz mentions food and sleep, I almost want to cry with relief. The king's hut is warm, and I could easily curl up on the floor next to the fire in the corner of the room. Terex gestures for us to follow him, and we make our way out of the hut and walk along a path of large tents, which he refers to as kradis. He stops in front of one of them, and a head immediately pokes out.

"I heard you were coming," an old woman says. "I prepared accordingly. Come in."

There are three women in the kradi, and it smells like flowers and herbs. A fire burns in the center of it, ensuring it's cozy and warm while the smoke escapes through a small hole cut into the top of the kradi. My eyes are immediately heavy-lidded, and Terex reaches out, grabbing my shoulder as I stumble.

The woman who greeted us gestures for us all to sit on rugs near the fire.

"I am Moni," she says, "and this is Talou and Fenri."

We introduce ourselves, and Moni turns to me while Talou and Fenri murmur quietly to the others.

Moni's green eyes study my makeshift sling. "We will need to remove this, child," she says, and I swallow around the lump in my throat at the sympathy in her voice.

Terex sits behind me and gently unties the sling, carefully removing it while I hold my arm at a ninety-degree angle.

Moni glances at Terex, and he moves closer, a knife in his hand. My heart almost stops, but he simply uses it to slice the sleeve of my pajama top, cutting away the material until it falls, revealing my poor elbow.

It's bruised and swollen, and I still can't move my arm at all without vicious pain.

Moni touches my arm and hums, studying it silently for a long moment. She gestures to one of the other women, who passes her a bowl of what looks like green mush. I flinch as she slathers it on my elbow, crying out as I hurt myself with the movement. Terex moves even closer, placing his huge hand over mine where I'm clutching my wrist.

"Gently, Ellie," he murmurs, and my heart flips at the way he says my name even as I fight back tears at the pain.

Whatever is in the green paste starts burning, and I cry out again. I want to pull my arm away and wipe off the paste, but I know any movement will make it hurt worse.

"Be at ease, child," Moni says. "You can't have healing without pain. Perhaps this is something that you have been slow to learn, hmm?"

She looks into my eyes for a moment, and it's as if she's looking directly into my soul. I shiver, and then the moment's gone, and the burning begins to ease, my elbow going numb beneath the paste.

Moni examines it again, giving a pleased hum at whatever she sees. Then she reaches for a piece of clean material, expertly folding it into a much better sling than the one I had. She pins it in place, and just like that, I can once again think past the pain.

"Thank you," I say, and she simply smiles and nods at me.

"Think about what I said."

Moni hands Terex some cream to put on my feet once I've cleaned them, and then I watch as the others are fixed up. Vivian had a deep cut along her back, which she'd kept to herself, and Nevada's knee has swollen to twice its usual size. Alexis's ankle is sprained, but by the time we leave the healer's kradi, all of us are feeling much better than when we first walked in.

Terex waits until the others are a few feet away and then draws me close. "I want you to sleep in my kradi, tiny female. What will it take to make this happen?"

I stiffen. "Are you making fun of me?"

Terex frowns. "I don't understand. I find that I do not want to let you out of my sight. Will you stay with me?"

I pull away, suddenly furious. "Did Vivian put you up to this? What did she offer?"

He glowers down at me. "Enough," he snaps.

I blink, stepping back.

"You are behaving erratically, likely because you are tired and hurt. I am willing to be patient, but you will sleep where I can see you."

I blink up at him, completely and utterly confused. The world is dancing around me, and I'm so tired that I must be hallucinating.

Terex takes my silence as agreement, and once again, I'm treated to his heartbreaking grin. "Come, female, I will give you food, and you will sleep."

His voice is low and pleased, and I sink into it as he leads me toward his kradi while I practically sleepwalk behind him. It's only when he opens the flap to his kradi and gestures me inside that I freeze.

What am I doing?

Terex glances at me. "Ellie?"

"I don't think it's a good idea to sleep in here."

"I will not hurt you, tiny female. I vow on my honor. I simply find that I wish to see you safe and content for the night."

"Terex..."

"What do you want? I will bargain with you."

I stare at him. I want him. I want to feel like this isn't a dream and a guy like him could possibly want me as a woman, not because he feels sorry for me and sees me as some sort of pet, or because someone has convinced him to play with me for a while.

I sigh. I want other things too.

"I want to find Charlie," I say.

"One of the females. The one with the head injury?"

"Yes. I was watching the fight. It wasn't a Voildi that took her. She was hurt, but she was tough. She would've fought back or made some sound if she could."

I'm suddenly hit with guilt. We should've stayed and searched longer. What if it were me, abandoned by my friends?

Terex examines my face. "We searched the surrounding area, Ellie. We searched a greater area than she would have been able to travel alone, and we looked in any places she could have hidden if she were scared. Staying would have been useless."

I nod. "Well, either way, she's out there somewhere. Nevada's right, and if she's going after the other women, I want you to help me find Charlie."

Terex studies me for a moment longer and then nods. "If this is what you wish, I will make it happen. I will help you find your friend, and you will stay in my kradi."

I eye him. "I'm not having sex with you."

His eyes widen and then darken, the violet turning a deep purple. "When we tumble, it will not be because of a bargain," he tells me. "It will be because you have begged to feel me inside you."

I blow out a breath. Oh boy.

CHAPTER FIVE

T*erex*

I LEAD THE TINY FEMALE INSIDE MY KRADI, TRIUMPH FILLING me as she sighs, immediately moving toward the fire. My kradi is large as befitting my status, and I am proud to provide Ellie with comfort and warmth.

Her large eyes examine her surroundings, and I almost smile as they dart from my furs on one side of the kradi. She is a nervous female, and while I don't understand why, I am willing to be patient.

I will wait for her to be ready to tumble with me. Even if it feels like the wait will kill me.

I muse over that as Ellie explores my space, poking her head into the smaller room used for bathing. I have never felt this way about a female, never felt the need to keep a female close and ensure she is safe.

Ellie's gasp tells me that Arana has filled the bath, and I

smile as I make my way to where she is eyeing it with longing.

"Would you like to bathe or eat first?" I ask.

Her stomach rumbles, but she nods toward the bath. I will have food waiting for her when she is finished.

"You will need help getting undressed," I say, and she flicks me a look.

"No, I won't," she says quickly. She gestures for me to leave, and I almost laugh. Sometimes she is as skittish as a wild animal, and other times, she is quick to order me around, as if *she* is the warrior.

I raise my eyebrow at being ordered from my own bathing room. A blush rises to her face, but she stares back at me, her chin sticking out stubbornly.

"You are in pain," I try once more. "I will help."

"I'm fine."

I let out a low growl, and it is her flinch that convinces me to go. "You will call me if you need help."

She nods in relief, and I move toward the fire, where Arana has left enough food for a feast. She is well aware of a warrior's need for fuel, especially when returning from a hunt.

I attempt to ignore the sounds of clothing dropping to the ground and sit down, focusing on the fire instead. I am not sure why this stubborn, tiny female appeals to me so much, but I will keep her near until I know the answer.

I tense at her gasp, and then I'm on my feet as a tiny, pained sound reaches me. I'm in the bathing room in a flash, coming to a stunned stop as I meet Ellie's eyes.

She glares over her shoulder at me. "What are you doing? Don't look!"

I raise a shaking hand to my mouth and glance away, but

nothing will erase this vision from my mind. Ellie, turned away, her skin glowing in the candlelight, her lush ass naked as she attempts to remove her shirt.

It is the last part that snaps me out of my sudden daze.

"You are in pain," I growl. "I do not know why you are so shy with me, but you will allow me to help."

"God, what is wrong with you? I said I'm fine."

The frustration in her shaky voice hits me, and I turn back to her, careful to keep my eyes on her face. It is flushed, her eyes filled with tears, and she is swaying with exhaustion.

"Enough," I snap, striding forward.

She flinches away, but I slide one hand around her waist, careful to keep my attention on the knot she has been struggling with.

"You should have called for me instead of hurting yourself," I growl. "Your stubbornness has only caused you more pain."

She lets out a rough breath but chooses not to reply, and I have the knot free within moments. I gently remove the sling holding her arm in place, and Ellie clutches her wrist, keeping her elbow still.

"Keep holding your arm right there," I tell her, moving around to the front of her body.

Her eyes are still filled with tears, and she glances away as I fumble with her shirt, cursing.

She lets out a tiny laugh, finally meeting my eyes. "You can rip the shirt if you want. It's just a rag now."

I do not want to risk jostling her arm, so I pull my knife from my belt and cut through the material. I do the same at the top so that she will not need to move her injured arm at all.

This alien female is incredibly shy with her body, and while I do not understand it, I must make allowances for her strange ways. I keep my eyes on hers as I take the elbow of her good arm and direct her to the bath.

I hold her and make sure she does not slip, and finally, she is sinking into the steaming water. A sigh escapes her, and my whole body tenses. I want her to make that same sound while I bring her more pleasure than she could imagine.

"Tell me when you are almost finished, and I'll help you wash your hair."

Ellie nibbles her lip, but her desire to be completely clean must outweigh whatever concern she has about my presence because she nods, eyes once again darting away until I leave.

I have a sudden vision of joining her in the large bath, coaxing her onto my lap and watching her eyes darken as she rides me. One day, she will not fear me.

Ellie

Terex finally moves back to the fire, and I sigh. That was mortifying. He's in such incredible shape, and knowing that he just stared at my naked, wobbly white butt is enough to make me want to cry.

I frown, confusion hitting me as I sink deeper into the warm water. I expected his touch to be clinical as he helped me, obviously too much of a gentleman to put up with a woman in pain. But his eyes were dark, muscles tense, and I didn't miss the lust on his hard face when he first walked in.

Could he really want me?

I find it difficult to believe, but if I judge him by his actions...

He's insisted I stay with him and helped me undress, and he seemed unwilling to put up with my pain. Then there's the comment he made about "tumbling" me.

The thought makes my cheeks heat, but I can't deny that the idea of Terex wanting me...

No, Ellie, you've made this mistake before.

The water is beginning to cool. I clear my throat, calling for Terex so he can help with my hair.

He instantly appears, a large jar in his hand as he moves toward the bath. "Dunk your head, tiny female."

I keep hold of my wrist, holding my elbow steady, and take a deep breath before sliding down enough to wet all my hair. I'm overdue for a cut, but I haven't had the time between teaching and volunteering.

Terex makes a pleased sound as I sit back up, and he reaches for my hair and squeezes it to remove some of the excess water. Then I feel something cool on my head, and he begins lathering it up, scrubbing my scalp until I'm almost purring.

"Your hair is beautiful," he says, and I smile in pleasure. It's the one physical trait that my sister was jealous of, her own hair thin and dry.

"When I first laid eyes on you, I imagined brushing this hair in front of my fire," Terex continues, and I shiver as his fingers continue to work the soap through the strands. "Will you allow me to do this for you?"

I'm no dummy. Drying and brushing my hair is a nightmare, especially without a hair dryer. Not to mention, my arm isn't likely to make the task possible.

"Sure. Um, that would be awesome. Thanks."

He helps me rinse and then washes my hair once more until it smells clean and sweet and the water around me is a dull brown.

"Ew." I wish I could rinse off in a shower, but I'm still a hell of a lot cleaner than I've been in days.

"Wait here," Terex says. He returns almost at once with a long, wide piece of cloth and gestures for me to stand.

"Um."

His eyes are stern. "I will not look. Are all humans so shy with their bodies?"

They are if they've been tormented like I was. "We're all different, just like you guys."

"Well, you have no need to hide your body from me. I have told you I will not tumble you until you ask me to."

He frowns at me as if I'm doubting his honor, and I sigh. "Terex—"

His eyes darken. "I like my name on your lips, tiny female. Now, step out of the bath before the water is cold."

I take a deep breath, but he's true to his word, keeping his eyes on my face as I get to my feet. He holds the cloth up in front of him while I step out, and I make him look away while I take it from him, pulling it under my elbow in an attempt to wrap it around me toga-style. I quickly realize that this is impossible with one arm and blow out a frustrated breath.

"Can you—"

Terex immediately recognizes the problem and helps me wrap the cloth around me. My hair is dripping, and he wrings it out over the bath and then reaches for another piece of material, gently patting my hair and removing the excess water.

Then he drops to his knees in front of me, drawing a squeak from my throat.

"What are you doing?"

"Drying you, tiny female. Will you allow this?"

I sigh, realizing that I can't do it myself, and I'm so tired I have almost nothing left in my tank. Maybe if I think of him like a doctor, it won't be so bad.

"Fine."

I keep my eyes on the wall of the kradi, ignoring his hum of approval. He's quick and methodical, patting the cloth along my body while keeping it mostly wrapped around me. He starts at my legs and moves his way up, making sure to dry the insides of my thighs. I wince as the cloth swipes over my chafing.

"I know, Ellie. I have more salve, but for now, we must make sure it is dry."

By the time he makes his way up to my breasts, butterflies are having a party in my stomach, and my nipples are hard, poking through the cloth.

He curses, low and rough, and heat sweeps up my cheeks.

"You are gorgeous."

I drop my eyes to his, stunned, and his eyes are dark as he looks up at me. I bite my lip, and his gaze immediately lowers to my mouth.

He seems to shake himself and gets to his feet, moving back toward the fire and then returning with a huge piece of fur.

"I will find you clothes in the morning, but for now, we can wrap this around you," he says.

He helps me into it, and I attempt to ignore the feel of his hands dancing over my body. They're strong and sure, warm and gentle. I sway closer to him, wanting nothing more than to curl up against his hard chest, and he ties the fur so that I can at least take small steps.

"Poor, tired female," he says. "Soon you can sleep."

My eyes widen, and I catch myself taking a step back as he leans over and picks up a jar I've seen before.

The scary paste that Moni used. The one that made me feel like my arm was being broken all over again before it finally went numb.

I narrow my eyes at Terex. "Moni already did that."

"And she told me to make sure we reapplied it before you went to sleep. Be brave, tiny female. It's for your own good."

I grind my teeth at his patronizing tone, but there's no denying the fact that while it hurts like a bitch, whatever is in that magic paste has also massively decreased the swelling and even briefly numbed my elbow before I started moving it while trying to get unchanged.

"Fine."

Terex steps aside and gestures for me to move in front of the fire. I sit on one of the large cushions close enough that I can feel the heat of the fire on my face. My eyes instantly attempt to slide closed.

"Ah, Jesus Christ, give a girl some warning!"

My arm erupts in fire, and tears spring to my eyes, but Terex holds my wrist, jaw firm. Within moments, my injury is blissfully numb once more, but I scowl up at him anyway.

He grins at whatever he sees on my face and leans down, pushing my damp hair off my face. "There, all finished. Now you can have your reward."

The heat in his eyes leaves no doubt as to the kind of reward he'd like to offer, but he moves away before returning with a comb in his hand. He helps me back into my sling and then positions his huge body behind me, encouraging me to lean against him while he begins working the knots from my hair.

I can't help but ask. "Did you really want to brush my hair when you first saw me?"

He pauses and then resumes his brushing. "I don't lie, tiny female. And never to you."

CHAPTER SIX

E*llie*

I WAKE WITH A JOLT. WHERE AM I? I'M WARM AND COZY, BUT my elbow is howling at me, not pleased by my sudden movement.

"Relax, tiny female. You are safe."

Safe.

I mouth the word to myself while I frown. I'm lying next to Terex, his warm body at my back and the warmth of the fire at my front. I'm leaning against a mound of pillows, and my heart flips as I look around. Terex has created a cocoon for me, making sure I'm sitting up slightly. He's also pushed pillows up against either side of me so I wouldn't roll onto my arm in the night.

Aw.

My stomach is screaming at me. My last memory is the feel of Terex brushing my hair, and he must have figured it was better to let me sleep. I could definitely roll over and sleep for a few more hours, but I'm so hungry I feel nauseous, and my stomach growls loudly at the thought of food.

Terex sits up and raises an eyebrow at me, obviously amused. "Such a fierce sound for one so small," he says, and I glower at him.

"Feed me, and I'll let you live."

He tilts his head back and laughs, and I stare at him, stunned. It's not fair that this guy is so gorgeous.

I attempt to keep my eyes off his chest, but that lasts about three seconds. Within moments, my eyes drift back to the play of muscles, which flex and roll as he moves. He's not wearing a shirt, and the blue scales along his shoulders glint in the light of the fire. I open my mouth to ask him about them, but he's already moving, and a choked sound escapes me as I get an up close look at his toned butt.

"Put on some pants!"

Terex sends me an amused look over his shoulder, and if I didn't know better, I'd think he was posing for me. I grab the pants he wore yesterday from the floor next to the bed and throw them at him with my good arm, instantly squeezing my eyes shut as he turns to catch them.

Okay, I may have cracked one eye open, but so would any red-blooded woman.

It turns out his huge sword wasn't overcompensating for anything.

I force my eyes shut for real this time, waiting until I hear him pull on his pants before I open them again.

"Are you a virgin?" he asks suddenly, voice curious.

"No, I'm not a virgin, thank you very much."

But to be honest, sex hasn't been much to write home about.

"Ah. So just shy. Soon you will learn not to be shy with me."

No, I won't.

Terex hands me a plate, and I begin inhaling my food as if he's going to take it away. His eyes light with pleasure as he watches me, and he hands me a cup of water before reaching for a plate himself.

I groan as I bite into a piece of something resembling bread. It has a perfect crust on the outside, and it's still soft on the inside. I try a range of fruits and nuts, finding that I like the green fruits that taste similar to cherries.

"There will be meat at the morning meal," Terex says, and I nod, stuffing my face until my stomach no longer aches.

"Wow," I say finally. "I demolished that. I was starving, thank you."

"It pleases me to feed you."

I don't know what to say to that, so I nod, blushing as I turn back to the fire. "When can we look for Charlie?"

"When your arm is healed."

My mouth drops open, and I whip my head around, meeting Terex's eyes. "That's not what we agreed."

He frowns at me. "Did you think I would allow you to travel for days while in pain? What kind of male would I be to allow such a thing?"

"Okay, buddy, we're going to need to talk about the a-word. You don't *allow* me to do anything."

Now that I have food in my belly and I'm no longer actively fearing for my life, I feel a little more confident doing battle with this huge warrior. Even when he narrows his eyes at me.

"I am bigger than you and stronger than you." He shrugs. "I know how to ride a mishua, and you do not. I know which tribes will be willing to answer our questions and which will attempt to kill us on sight."

I grind my teeth even as frustration and helplessness shoot through me, and my shoulders slump. Terex sighs and kneels in front of me, waiting until I raise my gaze to his.

"I am not trying to make you sad, little female. I only care for your health. I will take you back to Moni, and she will say when you may travel."

I nod. Truthfully, I know I'm in bad shape. My muscles still ache, my inner thighs are still sore, and while my elbow definitely feels better, I'm going to need to wear the sling for a while.

A small bell sounds, and Terex turns, moving to the kradi's entrance. Murmurs sound, followed by a female's giggle and Terex's low laugh. A guy like him must be popular with the women around here. I didn't miss how the few women who were still outside last night ran their eyes over his body when he arrived back at camp, as if checking for damage.

Terex returns, a bundle in his arms. "I have clothes for you."

I blow out a breath in relief. While the fur is warm, I'm scared I'm going to trip over it, and I certainly can't leave the kradi while wearing nothing but a blanket wrapped around me.

Terex unwraps the bundle, laying a long dress on the bed. It's plain but a lovely blue color, and the material is soft when I stroke it. He places a pair of shoes on the ground.

"I looked at your feet last night. I believe these will fit. They are Moni's granddaughter's shoes until we can have some made that will fit your feet."

I sigh. "How old is her granddaughter?"

The corner of his mouth tips up in amusement. "She has seen seven summers."

These people are so large that I'm wearing kids' shoes. No wonder Terex seems to think he can tell me what to do.

I pull them on, careful of the bandages Terex helped me wrap around my feet. I'm grateful to have any protection from the unforgiving ground.

"I will get you some boots before we leave camp in search of your friend."

I smile at Terex, and he reaches out his hand, stroking it down my face. "Beautiful female," he says, and just like that, the spell is broken.

He's obviously playing with me, and I move away, reaching for the dress. "Can you turn around, please?"

Terex frowns at me. "What did I say, Ellie?"

"Nothing. I want to get changed."

"I will help you."

"I don't need your help."

His frown turns into a scowl, and he crosses his huge arms in front of his chest. My gaze instantly drops to his muscles, and I see amusement in his eyes when I meet them again.

"I thought we covered this last night," Terex says. "I will help you—"

"I said I don't need your help!"

Surprise flickers over his face before it hardens. "Fine," he says softly. "I need to talk to my king. I will return when I am finished."

I blink back tears as I turn away, and he curses, pulling on his shirt and boots. I open my mouth to say something— I don't know what—but he turns and leaves me alone.

Terex

I do not understand this human female. One moment she is gifting me with her sweet smile, and the next she is refusing my help.

I understand that she is shy with her body, but after last night, I thought we had got past that. With her arm causing her so much pain, she needs my help to get ready for the day.

I stalk through our camp, nodding to those who call to me. I do not have time to stop, and truthfully, my mood is too dark to provide the information our people want to know about these females.

I nod to the guard at Rakiz's door and knock, unsurprised when Arana opens it. Her eyes widen at whatever she sees on my face.

"Terex," she asks. "Are you well?"

"I am fine. I simply do not understand females."

She smiles, and I wish it were Ellie gifting me with her smile instead of her angry words.

"Believe me, we don't understand males, either. The fact that the two have managed to coexist for so many centuries, mating and loving each other through their differences, is a miracle."

I smile at her, bowing my head as Rakiz enters, and he nods at me, sitting in his favorite spot in front of the fire while Arana hands him his morning meal.

We both turn as an angry female voice hits us.

"I need to talk to him."

"You are not on the list."

"I don't give a fuck. Move your ass."

Rakiz's eyes widen, and he gestures for me to open the door.

Nevada stands in front of me, wearing a long green dress. There is no question that she is a beautiful female, but she looks entirely uncomfortable, pulling at the neckline even as she narrows her eyes at me.

"I want to speak to the king."

"Let her enter," Rakiz says, and I step aside.

Rakiz meet's Nevada's eyes, and tension fills the room. Then he lazily scans her body, and we all watch as a furious flush hits her cheeks.

"Are. You. Finished?" Nevada's tone is frigid.

Rakiz raises his eyebrow, and she tilts her head, gifting him a look that no female has ever dared to gift him before.

Rakiz gets to his feet, handing his plate to Arana, who watches with wide eyes. "You show no respect."

"I respect those who earn it. You've given me no reason to respect you so far."

Arana makes a strangled sound and backs out of the room as Rakiz flicks his gaze to her. No doubt the rest of the camp will soon know every word of this altercation.

"Tread carefully, female."

Nevada narrows her eyes and casts him a look of such disdain that Rakiz steps forward, reaching for her even as she backs away.

"I just found out that you sent a tiny group of men to look for our friends. Without me."

Rakiz nods. "Yes."

This answer seems to infuriate Nevada further, but she takes a deep breath even as her hands clench by her sides. "I told you I was going with them."

I almost laugh. These human females are creatures like we have never seen before. For a moment, Rakiz stares at Nevada in fascination before his face hardens. "*I told you* that we would discuss the situation. We may discuss it now, but I have made my decision. I have sent some of my best warriors to find your friends."

Nevada scoffs. "Five. You have a camp full of warriors, and you sent five of them after our friends."

"I do not need to explain my decisions to you. But since you seem unable to understand how this planet works, let me attempt to teach you. We currently have forces in the North, battling with a tribe that would come and take everything we have, including our lives if they could. We have Braxian warriors in the East, hunting the Voildi from our territory. If any of these warriors fail, or if an enemy is able to get past our defenses, our tribe will be attacked. Right now, we have just enough warriors to hold this camp. Even five warriors make that questionable. So perhaps you should be *thanking* me for sending my men into danger."

Nevada has paled at his words, but her face flushes again even as she stares him down.

I know Rakiz, and he would always have sent warriors after the females. Not just because females are a blessing for our tribe but because he would never allow a female to come to harm if he could prevent it. But Nevada does not know this.

"Thank you," she grits out. "But you knew I wanted to go with them."

Rakiz laughs, and I flick my gaze to him at the cold sound. For whatever reason, this female makes Rakiz behave unexpectedly.

"The day I allow a female to hunt Voildi is the day I will no longer be fit to rule this tribe. You would die within days. You have no knowledge of this planet and its dangers, and no understanding of exactly how much peril you would be in."

"You patronizing—"

Rakiz holds up a hand, and Nevada's eyes meet mine. Her hand twitches, and I have no doubt that if I were not here, she would attempt to strike my king.

She whirls and leaves, slamming the door behind her, and Rakiz looks at me.

"She would have hit me," he breathes, stunned. "What kind of females are these?"

"They are not all this way," I say. "Ellie would not hit you." I pause. "Unless she thought you were going to hurt her friends."

To my surprise, Rakiz is no longer furious. Instead, he looks...intrigued. It is no secret that our king has long wearied of his rule. But he is the best ruler we could have, and he would never leave our tribe to experience the slaughter that would come as warrior after warrior was challenged for the crown.

For the first time in a long time, Rakiz has a hint of interest in his eyes. Interest for something other than killing every Voildi on this planet.

He frowns after Nevada and shakes his head, finally reaching for his cold morning meal. He gestures for me to sit, and I take a seat near the fire, thankful for the warmth on such a chilly morning.

Guilt hits me. I should have added an extra log to the fire in my kradi. Ellie feels the cold much more than I do.

"Asroz told me where the females were found, and I sent Hydrix and his men to this place. Hopefully, they can find some trace of the Voildi that took them."

A muscle twitches in his jaw, and I sigh. We both know that the likelihood of finding the females alive decreases each day.

"These Voildi were unlike any I had seen before," I say. "They wore clothing that covered their limbs and seemed to work together seamlessly, quickly separating the females and disappearing."

Rakiz rubs his cheek, once again placing his morning meal to the side. "Asroz told me this. This is good news. I have not heard of such a pack. This knowledge will make it easier to find the Voildi that took the females."

He doesn't say what we're both thinking.

That by now, the females may already be dead.

CHAPTER SEVEN

E*llie*

I STARE INTO THE FIRE AFTER TEREX HAS GONE. WHY WAS I such a bitch to him?

He shouldn't have mocked you.

What if he *wasn't* mocking me? He's made no secret of the fact that he finds me attractive, and he doesn't seem like the kind of guy to be so hurtful as to mock a woman who's hurt and clearly out of her comfort zone.

What if he really finds me beautiful?

I almost push the thought away, but instead, I take it out and examine it.

Maybe the rules of attractiveness on Earth don't apply here.

When Matt started dating my sister, I was devastated. Devastated enough that I made the mistake of writing down all my feelings in my journal. When Amelia found it, she waited until the perfect time for everyone to hear my innermost secrets.

The moment she looked across the cafeteria at me, I knew. I'd looked for my journal that morning, and horror had hit me when I'd found it missing. I'd thought I'd hid it in the perfect spot, beneath a floorboard in my closet. But Amelia knew my hiding spot. She was always one step ahead of me.

That morning, I'd pretended to be sick so I could stay home, but my mother had had no patience for me, declaring me perfectly fine to go to school. When I'd tried to explain what had happened, she'd snapped and told me she didn't have time for my high school drama and that I needed to put on my big girl panties and fix it myself.

By then, my dad had already been in the ground for five years.

So the moment Amelia grinned at me from across the cafeteria and climbed on top of the table, I knew what was coming. I jumped to my feet as she reached into her bag and pulled out my bright-pink journal, covered in photos of Justin Bieber. And I turned to run— only to find that she'd arranged for two of her jock friends to hold my arms, keeping me still and present for her humiliation.

Nausea sweeps through me at the memory. After all this time, I can still hear the laughter, still taste the tears on my lips, still feel the squeaky linoleum floor under my feet. I stood there and wished for the ground to open up, for a fire to rip through the school, for *anything* to happen to make it stop.

It never stopped. For the rest of my high school life, I was *that* girl. Matt tried to talk to me a few times, but I always ducked away, even after he finally saw Amelia for who she was and dumped her.

At fifteen, I still carried baby fat, some of which I lost by college and some of which is just my body. The thought of the weird, fat, unpopular girl lusting over the most popular guy in school? Hilarious. To everyone. I even caught one or two of the teachers staring at me, not bothering to hide the smirks on their faces.

I jump as a shadow appears outside the kradi, clutching the fur to me as someone steps into the entrance.

Terex is at my feet in moments, kneeling as he pushes the hair off my face. "Ellie," he says. "What's wrong? Are you hurting?"

I burst into tears, ugly crying even as he pulls me into his arms, careful of my elbow.

"I'm sorry," I sob, wetting his shirt. "I was mean and rude and immature."

"*I'm* sorry," he growls. "I should not have left you. What happened to make you so upset?"

He pulls away and sweeps his gaze around the kradi as if searching for a problem to fix. He glances at the dress and raises an eyebrow. "You didn't like the dress?"

I let out a hiccupping laugh, and his shoulders relax slightly.

"No, the dress is fine."

"What is it that has made you cry? You will tell me, and I will fix it."

I blow out a long, shaky breath. "You called me beautiful."

Terex tilts his head, confusion dancing over his handsome features. "This is...an insult to humans?"

I smile, and his gaze instantly drops to my lips.

"No. I'm just not used to men finding me attractive."

Terex narrows his eyes at me as if he's convinced I'm lying. "Are the males on your planet blind?"

I laugh, wiping at my face. "Well, you're good for my ego, that's for sure. I've...never had much luck with guys. I was bullied in high school for daring to have a crush on the most attractive boy in the school. When I finally escaped to college, my self-confidence was at an all-time low, and I buried myself in books."

I sigh, frowning as I stare into the distance. "You know... now I think I caused a lot of the pain myself by holding onto those feelings for longer than I should have. I let my sister give me this hang-up, that I was too awkward and ugly and no one would ever want me, and I played by those rules my whole life."

Terex scowls at me. "How could you think such a thing?"

I sigh. "Oh, if only you knew. Anyway, I tried to get the dress on for about five minutes, and I just couldn't do it. Will you help me, please?"

Terex's scowl deepens, but he allows the change in subject. I doubt he'll allow it for long though. He nods slowly, helping me to my feet. I pretend I'm not watching the way his muscles move while he grabs the dress and brings it to me.

I hesitate, clutching the fur to my chest while he patiently waits. Then I pull it up enough that he can help me step into the dress.

Terex holds the dress at my waist while I hesitate once more. This is ridiculous. I'm going to have to lose the fur.

I take a deep breath and drop the fur, standing before him, breasts bared as I shake like a leaf.

His gaze never drops from my face, but he smiles.

"Brave female," he says, and I feel my cheeks redden as he helps me pull up the dress. He gently unties my sling, and I tuck my boobs into the dress as he pulls it up at the back.

"This dress will work with your sling, but it will leave your arms bare. I'll find you a cloak to keep you warm."

There are thick ties on either side of my shoulders holding up the dress, and Terex gently maneuvers the ties around my arm, tying them and then replacing my sling.

The dress is way too long, dragging on the floor, and Terex frowns down at it, pulling out his knife. I step back and almost trip, and he grabs my good arm, turning that frown to me.

"What are you doing? Be careful."

"You can't cut it, Terex," I hiss. "It's someone else's dress."

He grins up at me. "Clothes have been donated for our new females," he says. "We have all noticed the size difference between our people and yours. No one would expect you to wear a dress you could trip on."

I bite my lip but let him cut away the excess material along the bottom of the dress. I'm sure it could be hemmed, but I can't currently do it, and I'd never expect someone else to do it for me. These people found us in dirty, torn pajamas, and they immediately offered us clean water, food, and clothes.

Terex uses his knife to roughly cut the bottom of the dress until it hits just below my ankles before he helps me put on my shoes. Then he gets to his feet and nods.

"Thank you," I say.

A growl leaves his throat, and he leans forward, one hand reaching into my hair to hold me still as he takes my lips with his.

I let out a startled gasp, and his tongue immediately finds mine, conquering my mouth like the warrior he is.

He tastes like berries and feels like heaven against me, his hard body cradling me as he gentles his kiss, his lips playing with my mouth until I tentatively kiss him back, my body going pliant as I clutch his shirt, pulling him closer with my good hand.

Terex groans, his hand finding my lower back as he pulls me closer, and my knees go weak at the feel of him hard and thick against me.

The sound of a bell makes him tense, and he curses as he pulls away. I feel dazed and overheated as I stare up at him, and he smiles gently down at me before stepping back and moving toward the entrance to his kradi.

"Thank you, Fini," he says, taking a tray. I catch a pair of curious eyes glancing at me, and then the woman nods, disappearing.

"Come, Ellie. Have some more food."

My mouth waters as an incredible aroma hits me, and I sit next to Terex by the fire. I'm still coming to terms with our kiss. It made my head spin, made the entire world fall away as if it was only the two of us.

I want to do it again.

"Ellie?"

Terex's voice is amused, and he looks very pleased with himself, grinning at me as he hands me a plate. I narrow my eyes at him, and his grin simply widens. Yeah, he knows I liked the feel of his lips on mine.

***

TEREX

I WATCH ELLIE EAT, THINKING ABOUT WHAT SHE TOLD ME. SHE lets out a tiny moan as she slides a piece of meat into her mouth, and I'm instantly hard even though I just managed to regain control of my body.

I cannot imagine a planet where males are not fighting to the death over my tiny female. I already regret the need for her to ever leave my kradi, where other males will stare at her dark eyes, long hair, and pleasing curves and attempt to coax her from my side.

I scowl at the thought.

"Terex? Is everything okay?"

"Yes," I say, shaking off my dark thoughts. I will take Ellie to Moni, and she'll tell us when Ellie is able to mount a mishua again. I understand that these females need to find their friends, and I will help them any way I can. But Ellie's health comes first.

Ellie leans back, patting her stomach. "That was delicious. I don't know what it was, but I'm stuffed."

"I will take you back to the healer now, and then you will rest."

Ellie raises an eyebrow, and I frown at her. Have I said the wrong thing?

I think over my words. "I would like you to rest so that you may heal and we can look for your friend Charlie."

Ellie smiles at me. "Okay, that sounds good, but I need to talk to my friends too."

I nod, placing our plates on the tray to be collected later, and lead Ellie out of my kradi.

The camp is bustling now. My kradi is further from the areas where most people gather, but the crowds of people pretending to be busy talking to each other make it obvious they're desperate to get a glimpse of these human females.

I reach for Ellie's hand, and my shoulders straighten as she threads her much smaller fingers through mine, allowing me to lead her to Moni's kradi.

"People are staring," she mutters, hunching her shoulders.

"It is just because you are new and different to the Braxian people," I say. "Soon they will be used to seeing you every day."

Her eyes examine my face, and she frowns at whatever she sees but slowly nods.

Moni smiles at us when we arrive, gesturing for us to sit. "How are you feeling today? I have already seen your friends."

"I'm feeling much better, thanks. How are the others?"

"They are doing much better as well. Now let me take a look at your arm."

Ellie sits quietly while Moni examines her, wincing slightly but allowing her to apply more of the healing paste. "When will I be able to leave?"

Moni's gaze flicks to mine, and I sigh.

"We are hoping to find news of one of Ellie's friends. The female was injured and disappeared during the battle."

Moni nods and finishes tying Ellie's sling. "Depending on how you feel, you should be able to sit on a mishua within one week."

Ellie's chin juts out stubbornly. "That's too long. Anything could have happened to Charlie in a week."

Moni narrows her eyes, unused to even the most hardened warriors arguing with her decrees.

She opens her mouth, and Ellie shifts, tears filling her eyes.

"Please," she says. "She must be terrified, and she's all alone. *We're* all alone on this planet. We need to stick together."

Moni sighs, glancing at me. I school my face, hoping she won't see how the tiny female's words sting. She is not alone on this planet. She has me.

I frown at these thoughts. For years, I have let females

come and go, even in a tribe where we have so few available. I never found the one I wanted to spend every night with, to raise children with, to grow old with.

Ellie is that female.

But she will leave. She will leave you as soon as she finds her friends.

My frown deepens. These humans have made it clear that they wish to return to their planet. I do not understand how they will do so, but I do know that if such a thing is possible, these stubborn, determined females will make it happen.

Not if you convince Ellie to stay.

I mull over that thought while Moni and Ellie stare at each other silently.

Finally, Moni huffs out a laugh. "Fine," she says. "Three days. But you must stop for frequent rests. And," she says as Ellie gets to her feet with a grin, "the healing salve three times a day."

I laugh at the look on the tiny female's face at that decree, but she nods. "Thank you."

"You are welcome."

Ellie

Terex leads me to another kradi and rings the tiny bells hanging at the entrance.

A head pokes out, and I grin as Alexis reaches out and grabs me in a hug.

"There you are. We wondered where you were."

"I'll be back soon," Terex says, and I nod, following Alexis into the kradi.

"Where are Nevada and Vivian?" I ask.

"Both of them disappeared to find different clothes. Nevada wants something she can 'move and fight in,' and Viv wants something that shows off her figure." Alexis gives me a look, and we both burst into laughter.

"Where'd you go last night? We turned around, and you'd disappeared, and all they'd tell us was that you were safe and in this camp."

I blush. "Terex wanted me to sleep in his kradi." I groan as Alexis laughs.

"Bow chicka wow wow," she says, and I can't help but grin at her antics.

"It's not like that. Don't look at me like that. It's not. We made a deal. For whatever reason, he wanted me to sleep in his kradi, and he said if I did, he'd help me find Charlie."

Alexis's grin falls at the mention of Charlie, and she nods. We're both silent for a moment.

Alexis sighs. "God, I hope she's okay. She was a firecracker, you know? The first to suggest we could take on those assholes who abducted us."

"She's okay," I say. "We have to believe that."

If I let myself picture her lying dead in the forest somewhere, or imagine the others being eaten by the Voildi...I won't be able to get up in the morning. We need to keep functioning so we can find them.

"I'm going with you," Alexis says. "I was standing next to Charlie before Terex and his friends appeared. If I'd paid more attention, I would've noticed when she disappeared."

I sigh. We all feel guilty. I've examined every moment of those few minutes in my mind, thinking up ways they could've gone differently.

"So you and Terex, huh?"

I laugh, and for a moment we're not two human women

abducted by aliens and trying to get off a strange planet. We're just two women gossiping about men.

"Yeah. Well, I dunno."

"What do you mean you don't know? Did you bang?"

"No!"

Alexis looks disappointed. "Did anything happen?"

I think of Terex's huge hands on my body, his lips claiming mine, and I shiver.

"It did, you dirty dog! Give me the details."

I tell Alexis about the kiss, and while she's disappointed it's "just a kiss," she glowers at me when I tell her all about my crying jag.

"He told you you're beautiful and you basically told him to fuck off and then cried?"

I groan. "It wasn't that bad. He wanted to help me get changed, and I thought he was mocking me. So I told him I could do it myself, and he got annoyed and walked out."

Alexis stares at me. "Poor guy."

"Poor guy?"

"Well, look at the man. That's probably not the usual response he gets when he tells women they're beautiful."

I scowl at the thought of Terex telling other women they're beautiful. "I didn't see it coming. He's...you know. And I'm...you know."

Alexis narrows her eyes at me. Then she reaches out and pulls my hair.

"Ow! What was that for?"

"For being an idiot. Why don't you tell me exactly what you mean by that?"

I scowl at her, getting to my feet to pace. "He's a huge, hot warrior built like a tank. I'm fat and average-looking at best. Ow, God, stop it!"

I slap Alexis's hand away.

"You," she says slowly, "are being ridiculous. First of all, if Terex thinks you're beautiful, who are you to try to convince him otherwise? Second, how do you get through life with such shitty self-confidence?"

I glower at her. "Not well," I mutter, thinking of the way I scurry my way through life in New York.

I sigh. "Look, my sister was a pageant queen. I'm talking gorgeous. She was thin and sporty and basically a spitting image of my mom. I got all my genes from my dad's side, and they never let me forget it."

Alexis nods. "I get it."

I tilt my head at her, unconvinced, and she raises one eyebrow. "You think you're the only woman to be told some next-level bullshit about the way she looks? Join the club. The difference is, I grew out of those terrible teenage years, and now I let that shit roll off my back. By believing you're unworthy of love and affection, you let them win."

I sigh again. "Easy for you to say," I mutter. "You're gorgeous."

She rolls her eyes, leaning back on the cushion, and scans her gaze over my body. "Are you kidding me? You're all tits and hips. I've been saving for a boob job for years."

I stare at her, and she rolls her eyes again, and then we both turn as someone opens the kradi flap.

"Oh, hey, guys."

My mouth drops open as Nevada walks in...wearing leather pants.

Alexis bursts out laughing, and Nevada grins at her.

"Better, huh? These guys are idiots if they think I'm going to be fighting in a dress."

Alexis snorts. "I don't think they're expecting you to be fighting at all."

"Yeah. Silly men." Nevada gives me a look. "And what happened to you last night?"

"She had a slumber party without us. But the good news is that she's convinced Terex to go look for Charlie. I'm going with them."

Nevada doesn't even hesitate. "I'm going too."

"Going where?" Vivian ducks into the kradi, her mouth thinning into a narrow line when she notices me.

"We're going to find Charlie," Alexis says. "But someone should probably stay here in case these guys find the others."

Vivian nods. "I'll stay," she says, and I blow out a breath of relief.

The bells ring, and we all turn as Terex steps inside.

"Hello, tiny female," he says with a grin, his violet gaze steady on me. "Did you miss me?"

"Jeez," Alexis says, fanning her face. "If she didn't, I sure did."

I grin at her, trying to ignore the way Vivian's eyeing up Terex's huge body from where she's lounging near the fire.

He keeps his gaze on me, letting it dance over my body in a way that clearly tells me he likes what he sees.

"Yes," I say boldly, watching his eyes darken. "I missed you."

***

Terex

I leave Ellie sleeping in my kradi, pleased to see her resting and healing. She won't admit it, but she's still exhausted, quickly falling asleep almost as soon as she places her head on the pillow.

Then I make my way to Rakiz, ready for battle. I must convince him that I should be the one to go look for Ellie's friend.

I find him leaning against the entrance to his tashiv, staring into the distance. "This female is driving me to madness," he says when I arrive, not looking at me.

I frown and turn, my mouth falling open as I stare at the training arena. Our camp is always designed this way even though we move with the seasons. The king's hut is built overlooking the warriors as they train.

Today, there is little training happening. Oh, the males clash swords, but their movements are sloppy, all of them too busy staring at the female in warrior's pants as she attempts to pick up a sword that likely weighs more than she does.

"Gods," I say, and Rakiz nods.

Nevada manages to lift the sword, but it's too heavy for her, and she ends up letting it fall to the ground, clearly disgusted. One of the males calls out to her, and she puts one finger in the air, waving it at him in what is likely a lewd gesture.

A laugh escapes me, and Rakiz glances at me, unamused.

"I'm sorry, but how long do you think it'll take before she's challenging our warriors?"

Rakiz closes his eyes at the thought, and then we both watch as Asroz takes pity on her. He steps forward, offering one of the smaller, lighter training swords used for males who have not yet had their first hunt.

She nods at him, taking the sword and swinging it in her hand. It's a good size for her, and Rakiz curses beside me, although the corner of his mouth turns up.

"That female looks like she was born with a sword in her hand."

I grin, and we both watch as she stares at the young males training on the far side of the area, mimicking their movements.

Asroz steps forward, and she nods again at whatever he says, adjusting her hold on the sword. Rakiz narrows his eyes and then turns, striding back into his hut.

I let a low growl escape. Negotiating with Rakiz is difficult at the best of times, but something about that female puts him in a filthy mood.

I follow him inside and get straight to the point.

"I have promised my female that we will look for their injured friend who disappeared during the battle," I announce, and Rakiz takes a seat, leaning back even as a muscle twitches near his eye.

I sigh. This is unlikely to go well.

"You have declared your intent to mate with this female?"

"No."

"Yet you call her yours."

I sigh again. Rakiz may be king, but we are still friends.

"I believe she is," I say, sitting beside him. "I believe the Gods made her for me, and I can convince her to stay."

Rakiz raises one eyebrow. "Truly?"

I think of the way Ellie's eyes lit up when I found her in her friends' kradi today. "Truly."

He sighs, a low growl escaping as he gets to his feet. "You believe we can do without you?"

"You know I wouldn't leave this camp if I thought our people would be at risk."

Rakiz slowly nods. "What makes you think you can find this female?"

"We searched the immediate area for her, checking in every hiding place we could find in case she crawled away to hide while wounded. She was bleeding heavily when I first noticed the females, and she would not have gotten far alone. I will approach Dexar's tribe. He has scouts in the area, and they may have seen something."

Rakiz nods again, and I clear my throat.

"One more thing. Alexis, one of the other females, would like to join us. Along with...Nevada."

Rakiz's expression darkens at the reminder of the female currently training with our men. "You will need at least one more male with you for protection."

I nod. "Hexer is due to return any day now with his watch. There are five warriors with him. We must wait until Moni says Ellie can travel anyway. I would like to take two more males with us—one for each of the females."

Rakiz is silent for a long moment, his gaze flicking toward the training arena once more.

"Fine. You can leave as soon as Hexer returns."

CHAPTER EIGHT

E*llie*

Two days later, Moni finally gives me the all clear to travel. My arm's still in a sling, but my elbow feels much better. So much better that I'd love to know what exactly is in that terrible green salve. On Earth, I'd likely be in a cast or something, yet now my arm feels good enough that I'm no longer treated to stabbing pain every time I do something simple like get changed.

Terex has been the perfect gentleman, helping me in and out of my clothes. He hasn't kissed me again, but his eyes drop to my lips enough to make me think he wants to.

I'm not sure why he's hesitating. Maybe he's waiting for me to make the first move this time?

I let my gaze drift over his body as he gets his mishua ready for travel. Deraz and Asroz are coming with us, and they're saddling up their mishua—Asroz explaining the process to Nevada, who's nodding as she listens intently.

She asked for her own mishua but was told that the beasts don't tolerate females riding them unless they're tethered to another mishua and the trip would be too long. Nevada's eyes narrowed in challenge as she stared at the mishua grazing in their pens, and Terex buried his face in my hair at her expression, his shoulders shaking with laughter.

Nevada seems to shock and amuse the Braxian people, who don't know what to make of a woman who wears men's pants and carries a sword. Alexis is becoming a well-known face in the kitchen, where she's learning about the different types of food here, while Vivian made friends with one of the seamstresses, loudly proclaiming that the dresses she created are the most attractive.

Yesterday, Terex gave me a tour, showing me the large communal areas where people gather to hang out, eat, and even bathe. The first thing I noticed? Men outnumber women ten to one.

"Why are there so few women here?" I asked Terex.

"We do not know. Something about this planet is inhospitable to females. All tribes struggle to continue their lines, with fewer females born each year. Our birth rates are low, and the Voildi continue to breed and breed."

I repeated this to Alexis, who frowned, muttering aloud.

"Something in the water? Some kind of nutrient deficiency? What could make this happen on an entire planet? And what do these guys mean by the whole planet? It's not like they have great technology. Do they actually know if this is happening everywhere? Or just in their corner of their world?"

I shrugged, leaving her to her muttering.

"You ready?"

I turn to find Nevada grinning at me. "Yup. Terex found

me some more clothes, and he said he's got everything else we need. You look happy."

She nods. "I am. It's a relief to be doing something, you know?"

"I sure do. Do you really think we'll find them?"

"I *have* to believe that we'll find them. I won't give up on them."

Her confidence is infectious, and I nod as Terex returns, ready to lift me onto the mishua. It seems as if half the tribe has gathered to see us off, and even Rakiz is standing nearby, deep in conversation with Deraz.

Rakiz slaps Deraz on the back and nods to Terex and Asroz. Once everyone has mounted, his dark gaze scans us.

"Travel well," he says, and then we're moving, the mishua jostling each other, obviously excited to be out of their pen.

Terex leans forward, murmuring in my ear. "I brought some salve for you," he says.

"Oh, I have some too. Moni said I only need to use it twice a day now."

"Not that one. The one for between your thighs. I'd be happy to apply it for you later," he says, his voice low and suggestive.

I blush, squirming, and my thighs tense. The mishua snorts, and I force myself to relax.

"Actually," I say, "that's no longer a problem."

I lift my long dress, displaying a pair of his leather pants. I stole them and gave them to Nevada, who convinced one of the seamstresses to tailor them for me.

Terex growls behind me, and I laugh as I turn, meeting his eyes.

"I find I enjoy seeing you in my pants," he says. And then he finally brushes a kiss over my mouth, pulling me closer.

His lips fit against mine, tongue stroking, and I sigh against his mouth.

My eyes meet Alexis's, and she grins at me.

"Get a room," she mouths, and I laugh again.

I wish.

Sometimes, Alexis reminds me of Amelia, with her long, straight blonde hair and icy blue eyes. But then she'll make a hilariously vulgar comment or notice I need a hug, and I'm reminded that she's nothing like my sister.

Terex places a gentle kiss on my neck and then turns the mishua, following after the others.

Over the past few days, I've been obsessed with the idea of Terex's huge body above me, below me, behind me, basically any way I can get it. I fantasize about him, desperate to feel his hands on me. Other than our kiss that first morning, he's been careful, barely touching me. I don't know if it's because of my arm or if I weirded him out that day with my tears.

One thing is for sure: the moment I'm out of this sling, I'm going to seduce the alien warrior. As soon as we find Charlie and the others, we're going to be coming up with some plan to get home. And that means that I may only have a few weeks or even days with the man who makes me feel so much.

If we only have a short amount of time together, I'm going to make it count. I've never felt like this before. Sure, I've had crushes, but Terex is different. Terex makes me feel protected but also attractive and sexy.

I don't know what it is about him that makes me feel like he'd never hurt me, but from the moment I met him, I've felt safe.

I doze on and off throughout the day, slumped against Terex. While my pants make riding a lot easier, my muscles are still aching when we finally stop for the night. The guys set up our camp next to a long river. Nevada watches them start a fire while Alexis and I take off our shoes and paddle in the river, squealing at the cold water.

According to Terex, we're lucky we crash-landed here when we did. Any earlier, and we would've been walking barefoot in the frost when we left the ship. I shiver at the thought and splash some water on my face before we make our way back to camp.

"Tell me," Nevada says once we're all eating around the fire. "What do you think the Voildi have done with the other women?"

I tense at the thought, and Terex rubs my shoulders. He's sitting behind me, handing me the best parts of whichever beastie they caught earlier. The meat is tender and perfectly cooked, and I can't help but wonder if our friends are eating.

Or if they've been eaten.

I push that thought away, but I shake my head as Terex offers me more food. I'm no longer hungry.

Asroz clears his throat. "We've thought about this. Typically, the Voildi would see the females as fresh meat," he says frankly, and I blow out a long breath, trying not to puke.

"But these Voildi looked different." He frowns.

Deraz nods. "They dressed differently and appeared almost civilized."

"What does that mean?" Alexis asks.

Asroz shrugs. "Females are highly prized on this planet. If their pack leader is able to overcome his basic instincts, he could sell the females for more money than his pack could ever hope to see in their lifetimes."

I tense at the thought, and suddenly all I can hear is the

auctioneer on that horrible planet. All I can see is the amused, mocking eyes of the crowd as we're all sold.

"Let's hope that's the case," Nevada says, and Asroz nods.

"There are only so many places that females can be sold. If Rakiz was to learn of such a place..." He trails off, and Deraz laughs.

"He would send our best warriors to cut down every Voildi in sight and take the females for their own."

Nevada's face clearly says what she thinks of that idea, and Terex shifts behind me.

"Rakiz is committed to our tribe," he tells her. "We need females for it to continue to grow. But he is also a good male." His voice gentles. "He would never allow females to be abused."

Nevada scowls at him but turns her head, staring thoughtfully into the night.

***

Terex

I wake, my body tense with need as Ellie shifts beside me, wiggling her ass as she backs closer to my warmth.

I close my eyes as I attempt to get my body back under control.

The last few days have been torture with my tiny female so close. But I will not touch her until she is no longer in pain.

A small part of me is waiting. Waiting for Ellie to kiss me, to show that she truly wants me. I've caught her eyes drifting to my lips, her avid gaze dancing over my body when she thinks I'm not watching.

My Ellie is shy and uncertain. I find this curious and strangely adorable.

I will wait as long as she needs.

I groan as Ellie wiggles again, and then she turns over, careful of her arm. Thankfully, it seems to pain her less and less each day.

"Good morning," she says.

"Good morning," I reply, my voice hoarse.

She smiles at me, and I want to wake up like this every day. Well, perhaps not every day. Sometimes, I want to wake with my female's hand wrapped around my cock. Other days, I want to wake her by licking her cunt until she screams my name.

These thoughts are not helping my situation, and I close my eyes once more.

"Wow," Ellie says suddenly, and I almost groan again as her warm fingers stroke my chest. One finger dances along my shoulder, and I shudder against her.

"Are these sensitive?"

I open my eyes. Ellie is staring at the scales along my shoulders and upper chest, and her eyes widen as they darken.

"They change color?"

I clear my throat. "Our scales reflect our emotions. It is thought that our ancestors used them as camouflage."

Ellie dances her finger over my shoulder again, and I catch it with a growl. Her eyes widen, and then an entrancing blush rises along her cheekbones.

"Does that feel good?" Her voice is low, eyes curious.

"You have no idea how good, tiny female. Your hands on me..."

A tiny smile pulls at her mouth. It stuns me that this female seems to be completely unaware of her power over me. But from the mischievous look on her face, she's enjoying my reaction to her.

"Knock, knock, lovebirds."

Ellie rolls away and sits up, wincing slightly at the movement, and that is enough for me to regain control. My female has been harmed enough on this planet. My need for her can wait until she is no longer in pain.

"We're getting up now, Alexis," Ellie calls.

Within moments, Ellie has pulled on her clothes, sending me one more smile before she leaves me to get ready. I pull my pants on over my aching cock and then dismantle our small travel kradi, packing it away.

The day is long. This time, Ellie doesn't sleep but chats to me about the children she taught on her planet. Her stories make me laugh, and while I do not quite understand all the words she says, it's clear that she loved each of the children she taught.

"You could teach children in our tribe," I say suddenly, and Ellie's mouth opens in surprise.

"You have a school?"

"The children have lessons. The males must also learn to wield a sword, and the females must learn female tasks—"

"Oh God," Nevada mutters, and Alexis snorts.

"Female tasks?" Ellie sounds displeased.

Asroz grins at me, while Deraz lets out a bark of laughter.

"Yes," I say. "But all children must be taught their numbers."

Ellie frowns at me and opens her mouth, but all our mishua stop at once, growling and snorting.

"What's going on?" Nevada whispers.

"The mishua are highly sensitive. They know when we

are approaching danger. It is likely to just be some of Dexar's sentries, but we will be cautious."

Ellie nods, her gaze scanning the area in front of us. We encourage the mishua to approach, and within moments, we're surrounded.

Ellie

"I'm really getting sick of this planet," Alexis mutters as we stare at the huge warriors surrounding us.

"Preach," Nevada says.

These warriors look similar to Terex and his tribe members. None of them are wearing shirts, and I watch as Alexis checks them out, gaze lingering on their bulging muscles, while Nevada scans them with cool eyes, likely planning how to take them down.

"State your business," the leader says. His hair is lighter than any I've seen here, a dirty-blonde braided back from his hard face.

"We must talk to Dexar," Terex says, his voice low and calm.

"You have not sent a messenger to request a meeting," the warrior says, his eyes dancing over us and lingering on Nevada. She bares her teeth at him in a feral grin, and all five of the warriors look at her as if she's crazy.

"We did not have time. You and I both know that Dexar and Rakiz have formed an alliance. Do you wish to put that in jeopardy with your actions today?"

The warrior narrows his eyes. Obviously he's got something to prove, but he finally steps to the side, gesturing for us to move forward.

The mishua don't seem to like being surrounded by the warriors, and they're jumpy. Terex handles Kini expertly, and she finally settles down while we ride toward the camp in silence.

This camp seems to be larger than ours. Gazes follow us as we make our way toward the largest kradi, and we finally dismount. Terex helps me off the mishua, and they're tied to a fence close by and given water.

According to Terex, this tribe refers to their king as a qatai. The people are also Braxian, but this tribe has gradually taken over more and more territory, leaving smaller camps in place for months at a time to hold their vast lands.

The warriors lead us into the kradi, although the word doesn't seem appropriate for such a vast space. It reminds me of a massive circus tent with the ceiling far above us. The walls are decorated with jewel-toned fabrics, and lush carpets cover the floor. The kradi is sectioned so we're standing in an entranceway.

"Through here," the first warrior says, lifting one of the pieces of cloth.

The qatai sits in a huge, throne-like chair overlooking the large space. Cushions and chairs are filled with people who stare at us curiously, murmuring amongst themselves.

"Terex," the qatai booms, and the room goes silent.

Beside me, Nevada's hand slides toward her sword, her gaze scanning our surroundings.

"What are you doing?" I hiss at her.

"I have a bad feeling about this. Keep an eye out for any other exits."

On that cheerful note, I return my attention to the qatai.

"Dexar," Terex says, nodding respectfully. I raise an eyebrow, but the qatai doesn't seem offended by Texar's use of his first name.

"Who are these females you bring with you?" Dexar's dark eyes widen almost imperceptibly, and I move close to Terex as Dexar studies Alexis. She stares back at him boldly, and he raises his eyebrow.

He's huge. Bigger even than Terex. And while Terex is both a warrior and classically handsome, Dexar's face is all hard lines. His nose has been broken once or twice, he needs a shave, and while his lips are full, they're currently twisted wryly as his eyes scan us. I'd thought his eyes were dark, but as he steps closer, I see they're really a deep forest green.

Terex explains our situation, and Dexar's eyes widen in surprise as people begin to murmur around us again. Warriors line the walls, and I suddenly wish we brought more backup with us.

Surely Rakiz wouldn't have let us go if he thought Dexar would hurt us.

I cling to that thought, but something about the way Dexar's gaze lingers on Alexis makes me wonder how well Rakiz truly knows the qatai.

"During the battle, three of the females were taken by the Voildi. Rakiz has sent warriors to look for them. However, another female also disappeared around the same time. She was small and dark-haired."

Even I can tell when recognition hits Dexar's face. He knows something. Something about Charlie. I shift impatiently, and his eyes meet mine before once again landing on Alexis.

"What is your name?" he asks her suddenly.

"Why does it matter?" she frowns at him, and the entire room seems to collectively inhale before everyone goes silent.

He stares at her for a moment and then gives her a slow

grin. His grin transforms his face, turning him into a handsome man. "You wish for my help, and yet you won't tell me your name?"

Alexis flushes, shifting uncomfortably. "Alexis," she grits out.

"Alexis," he repeats, lingering over the word. His attention returns to Terex, and he moves back to his throne, regarding us with his dark eyes.

"Three nights ago, I received word from a group of my men stationed in the northeast corner of my territory," he says. "I was unsure what to make of their message, believing they must have had too much noptri that night. The female was wearing strange clothes that my men had never seen before and was bleeding heavily from her head."

"Charlie," I breathe, and Terex pulls me close.

Nevada shifts, narrowing her eyes at Dexar. "And?" she asks coolly.

"And I find myself unwilling to offer up such vital information without anything in return."

Terex tenses next to me, but it's Nevada that says what we're all thinking.

"You son of a bitch."

Dexar stares at her for a long moment and then gets to his feet.

"What do you want?" Terex asks.

"I want her," Dexar says, gesturing to Alexis. She pales, and a scornful laugh leaves Nevada's throat.

"You have *got* to be fucking kidding."

Dexar ignores that, keeping his attention on Terex.

"Your tribe has found three females," he says, and none of us correct him by mentioning Vivian. "You are searching for four more. You are well aware of our shortage of females."

Alexis looks disgusted, but she shifts, moving slightly behind Asroz, who glares at Dexar.

Dexar doesn't miss this, his gaze flicking back to Alexis.

"You would be safe here," he says. "I would see to it personally. No one would harm you, and I will give you the information needed to find your friend."

Alexis shifts, a stricken look on her face, and Nevada steps forward.

"What kind of person would ask something like this?"

"I am not a good male," Dexar shrugs. "Like most on this planet, I take what I want, and I do not apologize for it. You will need to learn this lesson well if you are going to stay here."

Nevada opens her mouth, likely about to declare that we're not planning to stay here, and I step forward, elbowing her in the side. She clamps her mouth shut and sends Dexar a withering look, but he's entirely focused on Alexis, who's scowling back at him.

"It's your choice," he says softly.

Alexis's eyes fill with tears, and she glances around, likely taking in all the people staring at us.

Dexar's voice rises slightly. "Out," he says, his eyes never leaving hers. People get to their feet instantly, moving from the room, and Nevada's eyes flicker over the crowd as a few people pull aside a different piece of material, revealing a hidden exit.

"What is your decision, female?"

"You won't give us the information any other way?"

He slowly shakes his head, and Nevada trembles with rage beside me.

I turn to Alexis. "Don't do it," I tell her. "We'll find another way."

Nevada nods. "Ellie's right."

Alexis blows out a breath. "What does this mean? What exactly do you want from me?"

Dexar shrugs. "I simply want you here, where I can see you."

Alexis wrinkles her nose, obviously not buying it. Nevada snorts, likely feeling the same.

"Just so we're clear," Alexis says, "I'm not sleeping with anyone."

Dexar grins, and once again, it changes his whole face. Something tells me that few people get to see this side of him. "I don't need to make a bargain with you for a tumble," he says. "Females beg me for this."

Alexis rolls her eyes, but relief is obvious on her face. "How long do I have to stay?"

Dexar's grin disappears, and his eyes focus intently on Alexis. "One revolution."

My stomach sinks as Alexis pales.

"Is that a year? How many days is that?"

"Two hundred and ninety."

We all gasp while Dexar simply keeps his eyes on Alexis, who is now so pale she looks like she might pass out.

"Charlie was really hurt, you guys." She hesitates, and Nevada glares at Dexar but moves forward, whispering something in Alexis's ear.

Alexis nods, a flash of relief on her face, and Dexar's eyes narrow.

"I want one more thing," Alexis says.

Dexar smiles, and I scowl at the triumph on his face.

"What?"

"Rakiz has sent a group of hunters looking for our friends, but they haven't returned. I want you to send some as well. But I want you to swear that if they find them, they'll return them to Rakiz's tribe."

The smile drops from Dexar's face, and he frowns at that. "Why would I do this?"

"Maybe you're not a good person," Alexis says, "but you don't have to be a bad one."

Dexar scowls at her, and she moves behind Asroz again. This seems to piss off Dexar further, and he steps forward. "Fine, female. Now cease hiding behind another male. I am the only male who will provide you with protection."

Alexis's eyes dart at that proclamation, but she nods. "Swear it."

Dexar nods. "You are a brave female," he says. "I swear that I will send my hunters to look for your lost friends, and if found, my men will return them to Rakiz's tribe."

Alexis sighs and then turns to us with a shaky smile. Nevada pulls her into her arms for a brief hug, and then Alexis reaches for me.

"We'll come back for you," I whisper, and she grins.

"You know, that's what Nevada just said. I'll see you guys soon." Alexis moves to Dexar's side, and then he turns to us.

"My men saw the female in the clutches of Dragix as he flew over the Seinex Forest."

Terex tenses, and Asroz's mouth falls open.

"Who's Dragix?" I ask.

"A giant beast who soars through the sky, breathing fire," Dexar says. "Our great ancestor."

I gulp. "You're telling me you guys are descended from dragons?"

Dexar frowns at me as if he doesn't understand my shock. "Yes. Dragix isn't truly our ancestor, but he is the last of the Great Ones."

Oh God. Charlie has been taken by a dragon. An alien dragon.

"How do we get her back?" I whisper, my lips numb.

Dexar shakes his head. "Attempting to find Dragix's lair is suicide."

"Why would a dragon take Charlie? She was wounded. Would he have eaten her?"

Dexar shrugs, and I want to punch him for the unconcerned look on his face.

"The Great One is covetous and possessive. Perhaps she was wearing something that caught his eye."

I swallow, trying to remember if Charlie was wearing a necklace or earrings. She didn't seem like the type to wear much jewelry, and we were all in dirty, torn pajamas.

A hush falls over the room, and I study the floor, depressed. Finally, Terex nods, clearing his throat. I meet Alexis's eyes, and she smiles nervously at me. I force myself to follow Terex out of the kradi.

CHAPTER NINE

E *llie*

We travel in silence until we're far away enough from the camp that Terex allows us to stop to stretch our legs.

Nevada stalks away and shrieks suddenly, kicking a rock. The warriors stare at her as she shrieks again, hands fisting as she turns to me.

"I'm so fucking sick of males on this planet! They've screwed us again and again and *a-fucking-gain*. Every species, from the Grivath who stole us to those purple assholes who bought us, oh—and the Voildi who wanted to eat us. Then we have the bastard back there who couldn't even give us the information we needed to find Charlie without screwing us over."

I turn to the guys and jerk my head, gesturing for them to give us some space. They move away, talking quietly amongst themselves.

"I know," I say. "But we have to focus on what we can control. Now we know where Charlie is."

"Oh yeah, now we just have to find a fucking dragon." Nevada laughs, and a tear leaks from her eye. I stare, stunned, panic making my palms sweat. Nevada never cries. Nevada's our rock. She's the one who has kept us all going. If she breaks down, how the hell will we get out of here?

"It's not ideal," I say slowly, "but Alexis made a choice."

"Alexis is a mechanical engineer. She's our best hope of getting off this goddamned planet." Nevada kicks a rock, a fierce scowl on her face, and even Asroz gives her a wary look.

A mechanical engineer. No way.

"Do you think she could fix the spaceship?"

"I have no idea. But she wanted to take a look at it. Now we're fucked."

"Okay, let me think." I wrack my brain furiously. "We can't do anything until we find the other women anyway."

Nevada nods. "If there's a chance we can get out of here and get to a planet where we can contact the Arcav, we can get home. But I'm not going without them."

I nod. "Me neither. Okay, so we know Alexis is safe, right? That huge asshole promised she wouldn't be hurt. That means that we just need to get everyone else together first. As soon as we have the other women, we can find a way to break Alexis out of that camp."

Nevada stares at me. "You've changed," she says. "And I like it." She blows out a breath. "Okay, you're right. Alexis chose to go so we could get information about Charlie. Now we just have to find the other women, save Charlie from a dragon, break Alexis out of that camp, and get our asses back to the ship."

We stare at each other, and I nibble my lip. "No problem."

"Yeah," she says. "Piece of cake."

Terex approaches and pulls me close, nuzzling my hair. "We were just discussing another option to find information about your friends," he says. "There is a camp just one day's ride from here. We can't all go—Rakiz needs me to return to camp. But Asroz and Deraz think they can make it by nightfall. We do not know the leader of the tribe well—he recently took over from his father. But they may have more information about the Voildi."

"I'm going with them," Nevada says, and Terex studies her.

"They will be taking no breaks. It will be a fast trip with no sleep."

"I can do it."

Terex nods, and Nevada turns to Asroz and Deraz.

"Let's go."

My head whirls as they gear up to leave. I don't like that we're all splitting up. "Are you sure you'll be okay?"

Nevada gives me an impatient look and then throws her arms around me, careful not to knock my arm. "I'll be fine. I'll see you back at camp. You know I need to be doing something, Ellie."

I nod. "Be careful."

Within moments, they're gone, and Terex and I are on our own.

"Are you okay?" he murmurs into my ear as lifts me onto the mishua and climbs up behind me.

"Yeah. I'm fine. Just worried about Alexis and everyone else, you know?"

"I will do everything I can to help you find your friends, tiny female."

I smile at his nickname for me. "I know."

We're mostly silent as we head back toward camp. We'll be stopping to sleep in the same area as last time, close to the river. For now, I'm content to lean against Terex as he points out animals I've never seen before and plants that look like they're out of a movie—all while we travel under a turquoise sky.

I had a quiet life in New York. After escaping my tiny town in Louisiana, I was swept away with the hustle and bustle of New York when I arrived—desperate to see all the attractions I'd dreamed of for so long. But once I started working, I fell into a routine, only leaving the city to go back to Louisiana when my mother convinced me she was sick or guilt-tripped me into visiting.

Agron is so different to anything I could have imagined on Earth. I've heard stories of Arcavia, and the technology the Arcav have provided humans with is incredible. But I forgot that there would also be alien races that are far less advanced than ours.

Part of me wishes that we crash-landed on a planet with the technology to contact the Arcav and get us home. But another part of me instantly rejects that thought because if I hadn't landed here...I never would've met Terex.

"Tell me about your life, Ellie."

I smile as Terex's strong arm tightens around my waist, ensuring I won't slip. I keep a death grip on the front of the saddle with my good hand, since I'm still not entirely used to the jolting movements of the mishua.

"Well, I live in a big city. Think of a camp that stretches over all the land we've ridden and into the distance, with buildings that rise into the sky."

Terex shifts. "It is almost impossible to imagine."

I smile, thinking of how surprised I was to learn about

the Arcav technology that they take for granted—like their ability to easily travel between planets.

"It does," I agree. "We don't have mishua, but we have horses, although people don't ride them to get to places anymore where I live. They mostly ride them for fun."

"Then how do you get from place to place?"

"Well..." I'm about to attempt to explain how cars work when the mishua suddenly stops, a weird sound leaving her throat.

Terex tenses. "Voildi," he growls. He jumps off the mishua, and my heart pounds in my chest as he stares up at me.

"Listen carefully," he says. "If I fall, you must cut this strap right here." He points to a piece of leather that's wrapped around the mishua's nose.

"This will tell Kini to return to camp," he says. "She will move quickly, so you will need to hold on as tight as you can, do you understand?"

I shake my head. "I'm not leaving you."

Terex bares his teeth at me, and I jerk my head back as he stalks closer.

"You will do whatever I tell you to do if it means your safety," he says.

I nod because he expects me to, but he obviously still knows nothing about human women if he thinks that I'd leave him behind.

Terex turns, scanning our surroundings. He leads the mishua behind him, and within moments we're surrounded by a pack of Voildi.

"Braxian scum. Traveling all alone so far from your territory? Time to die."

These Voildi look like the pack that found us on the ship. The leader's eyes meet mine.

"You look tasty," he says. "I bet your meat is tender."

Bile rises in my throat, and he laughs just as Terex leaps forward and slides his sword underneath his ribs.

It happens in an instant, and Terex immediately slides his sword free before swinging it again and beheading the Voildi within seconds.

I gag as the head rolls toward me, but I don't get a chance to puke because Terex is instantly attacked from all sides.

They're leaving me alone for now. Because they don't see me as a threat. The thought pisses me off, and I reach for one of Terex's knives, which is practically a sword in my hand.

"I need your help," I tell the mishua, who ignores me.

I kick her as if I was riding a horse, and she makes a dangerous sound, tilting her head to stare at me from one red eye. I remember Terex saying mishua refuse to be ridden by females.

"Whatever happened to the sisterhood? How about you do your girl a solid and help me help Terex?"

Kini ignores me, and my heart races even faster as Terex barely dodges an attack from a Voildi who managed to sneak up behind him.

"If you don't help me, I'm getting off. Terex will be *so* pissed at you if I die."

I swing one leg over, and the mishua finally moves, almost dislodging me. I squeak as I flail on her back.

"You did that on purpose," I growl.

A Voildi is backing closer to me, completely disregarding me, and I'm going to make sure it's the last thing he ever does.

These assholes would *eat* me if they could, and there are currently six of them attacking Terex. He's like a machine, cutting them down in blindingly fast motions, but I can see the strain on his face.

I lean forward, ready to jump on the Voildi's back, my knife clutched in my hand.

"Hey, asshole," I call. He turns just as the mishua jolts forward, and I bury my knife in his eye.

"Ew, ew, ew!" I pull it out, gagging as he screams, and then Terex is there, beheading the guy as he glares at me.

"What did I say?" he roars, then turns, gutting the first Voildi to rush him.

And then there are four. My hand is shaking, and blood drips from the knife. My mouth waters ominously, but I shake it off.

"You can puke later, Ellie."

I eye the Voildi. Now that Terex is guarding me more closely, I can't get to any of the others. Probably a good thing. The fact that I managed to stab the last one was sheer luck.

Terex punches one of the Voildi in the face, and the Voildi's nose explodes as Terex stabs another one with his sword. He pulls his sword free, but more Voildi are attacking, retribution on their faces.

Within moments he's down to three Voildi, but these ones are the better fighters. They've waited for him to get tired, letting their friends die first.

Shit.

They attack from all sides. Terex is larger and swings his sword like a man possessed, roaring a challenge. The first one to lunge forward is the first to die.

And then there are two.

They attack together, and I hold back a scream, unwilling to distract Terex as the Voildi leap forward. One of them slices at his leg, attempting to distract him while another leaps up and tries to take his head.

Terex guts the Voildi, snarling as his sword slides home. But that moment of inattention costs him, and I let out a shriek as the first Voildi darts forward and stabs him in the side.

I instantly know that it's bad.

Terex growls, pulling the smaller sword out of his side and stabbing the Voildi with it. We meet each other's eyes, the last of the Voildi choking and dying around him, and I shriek again as Terex falls to his knees.

Terex

Life is made up of moments. And the moment I allowed that filthy Voildi to stab me was the moment I lost my life.

I've fought many battles over my lifetime. I know when a wound is likely to kill me.

If we were back at camp...I have no doubt that Moni could heal me. Unfortunately, we are still many hours from home.

Ellie appears, kneeling beside me, sobbing. I didn't want to leave her like this.

"Get...on...mishua. Kini will...take you...back..." I run out of breath after that—closing my eyes for a moment.

"Don't be stupid! I'm not leaving you here. I have that green paste from Moni. Will it help?"

My eyes are heavy, but my face is suddenly warm, and I rouse myself enough to meet Ellie's beautiful eyes. "Did... you...hit me?"

I feel my lips curl. Fierce female. Sorrow fills me. We were supposed to have a lifetime together.

"Terex! Will it help?"

I shake my head and immediately stop as the movement makes pain explode in my side. "For bones."

"Okay." Even with my eyes closed, I know Ellie is biting her lower lip in that absent, sexy way she does.

I hear ripping, and a growl leaves my throat as she presses something against my wound.

"Jesus, there's so much blood, Terex."

More ripping. Is she tearing her dress?

"Kiss me...one last time...tiny female."

I crack open my eyes to find Ellie scowling at me.

"You're not dying," she declares even as tears run down her face. "You don't get any kisses until you're back at camp."

"Cruel female."

She's no longer listening, jumping up and rushing to the mishua.

"I need your help," I hear her say, and I almost snort. Mishua barely understand our language. The human language will be completely foreign to them. Unlike us, they have no translators in their ears.

"Ellie—"

"Are you listening, you stubborn beast? I need you to help me."

I crack open my eyes again as a shadow falls over my face. I don't know how much time has passed, but the mishua stares down at me, leaning down to sniff at my wound.

"Okay. Now we just have to get you on her back."

I blink, and then Ellie is above me, her face pale and streaked with tears. She slides her arm out of her sling, and the remaining color drains from her face. Then she leans down, staring me straight in the eyes.

"You're losing too much blood. If I can get you on the mishua, I can get you back to camp. But you have to help me. If you pass out, I won't be able to lift you. Do you understand?"

Her voice rises at the end as panic chokes her, and I nod. I can feel my blood beneath me, cooling on the ground. My chances of making it back to camp alive are not high, but if this is what my female wants, this is what I will do.

Even if it may kill me.

"Okay. How do I make Kini kneel?"

I snort. "Mishua...kneel for...no one."

Ellie scowls at me and then directs that scowl up at the mishua, who snorts at her.

Ellie clicks her fingers, gesturing to the ground as the mishua stares at us. "You know what we need, Kini. He can't get up that high."

The mishua lifts her head as if uninterested, but her gaze quickly returns to us.

Ellie gets to her feet, her eyes narrowing threateningly. I open my mouth as fear fills me. Mishua require respect and can become incredibly dangerous within an instant.

Ellie reaches for one of the Voildi's knives and points it at the mishua. "Kneel or I'll cut you open," she says.

I almost laugh even as terror makes my hand shake as I reach for her. This tiny female threatens a mishua that could lash out and kill her in half a second.

Unfortunately for Ellie, her threat likely doesn't come out as she intended it. Her voice is desperate, her words choked.

The mishua stares at her for a moment longer, and I open my mouth to beg her to run, and then I blink, stunned.

Kini drops to her knees, bowing her head.

I'm still attempting to understand this when Ellie nods. "Thank you," she says, then crouches next to me.

"Okay. I'm going to put my hands under your arms and pull. But I'm a weakling, and you're a giant. I need you to use those warrior legs and push back."

"Ellie," I try one more time, and she simply scowls down at me.

She will be carrying my body back to camp.

I nod. If this is what she needs, this is what I will do. I can deny my tiny female nothing.

Ellie leans down, and a sound leaves her throat. The kind of sound she should never have to make.

Her arm.

"Ellie—"

"Push, damnit!"

I gasp, spots appearing in front of my eyes as I manage to push backward, scooting to where Ellie directs me. My vision swims, and I close my eyes until my cheek stings again, then open them to see Ellie's pale, beautiful face.

"Terex!"

I blink up at Ellie. She's screaming, and I wonder how long I was out.

She moves her face closer to mine. "One more. One more, and you'll be on the mishua, and I can get you home."

Home. I would like to die with Ellie in my arms, my king at my side.

This will hurt.

I manage to make it onto the mishua, and Ellie somehow arranges my body so that I am slumped over Kini's neck, one leg on either side.

Ellie nods, and a sob escapes her as she leans forward, kissing me gently on the cheek. "Thank you for everything you've done for me, Terex. You saved my life. Now I get to save yours."

Adrenaline hits me as the mishua gets to her feet, and I realize what my tiny human is doing. She will not be able to reach the leather strap on Kini's nose while also on the mishua's back.

I open my mouth, and a roar leaves me. "Don't you *dare*—"

My stubborn female gives me one last watery smile and then reaches out with her knife and cuts the strap.

CHAPTER TEN

E *llie*

The mishua snorts at me.

Is she...laughing?

"You know the rules," I tell her sternly. "Get back to camp."

Terex growls—a low, dangerous sound that would make me shake in fear if he wasn't bleeding like a stuck pig.

"I am on her back...and she will...not leave without my order," he snarls. "Get up here. Now."

Terex has lost all patience with me, and I can't really blame him. I don't know how he expects me to get on the mishua's back now that she's standing, but I move to the side, staring up at him.

He holds out his hand, and I shake my head. I can't get up so far without him, and I'm not going to risk making him bleed any more than he already has.

Terex snarls at me, and I roll my eyes but finally follow

his gasped orders and stand on his foot as he hauls me up behind him.

He immediately passes out.

Honestly, I'm surprised it took him this long. I think his worry for me and sheer adrenaline must have been the only things getting him this far.

"That's fine," I say, my voice shaky. "At least he's not feeling any pain right now. Let's go, Kini."

Thankfully, the mishua listens this time, and she doesn't mess around. I hold on with my good hand, wishing I hadn't left my sling on the ground behind me as every movement jostles my elbow.

My arm is way better than it was, but dragging Terex's huge body around has done some damage. I'm lucky he was conscious enough to help me because there's no way I would have been able to get him on the mishua by myself.

Now that we're on our way back to camp, I give into the fear once more, shaking as tears run down my cheeks. My warrior is dying.

His blood...it was everywhere. I don't know how it's possible to lose that much blood and still be alive. Granted, he must have more blood than the average human given his size, but...

Kini increases her speed, and I wish I found a way to tie Terex to the saddle. I'm clutching him, but if he falls off, we're screwed.

The hours drag on. Terex occasionally groans, but he's unable to respond, so I pass the time by talking to him, likely driving him crazy with my chatter but hopefully giving him—and myself—something to cling to.

I tell him all about growing up in Louisiana with a mom who won Miss America before we were born and a sister who looked just like our mom and loved the pageant circuit.

"I hated it. I hated the big hair and the stupid dresses and being judged. I *loathed* being on stage, and I hated that my sister's old dresses never fit. They always had to be taken up and taken out, and my mother never failed to make me feel like it was my fault that I took after my father instead of her."

Terex groans, and I freeze.

"We're almost there," I lie. I have no idea how far away we are, but we haven't yet passed the river where we stayed that first night. I'm suddenly longing for Nevada and the other warriors. If we hadn't split up, this never would've happened. Terex wouldn't be—

"You're not dying. I know you think you are, but you're not. My dad had this saying: survival is 90 percent mental. I never understood it until this last week, but now I get it. If you give up, you're done. If you're going to go down, at least fight until the bitter end."

Terex groans again, and I choose to believe he's groaning in agreement.

"My sister always hated me. I was closer to our dad, and she loathed that we had more in common. I never understood the jealousy 'cause she and mom were so similar, you know?"

I chat for hours, focusing on the feel of Terex, warm and alive against me, and not the feeling of his blood dripping down the saddle.

I tell him about fourth grade, when Amelia hid rotten fruit in the bottom of my backpack and encouraged everyone to call me Smelly Ellie for the rest of the school year. Then I tell him about high school and how my dad had just died, and I was a social pariah after Amelia read my journal aloud. And then I tell him how at night I used to fantasize about going to sleep and never waking up.

We pass the spot where we camped the first night, and I blow out a breath. Kini has kept up a good pace—faster than I've ever experienced while riding her.

"Then what happened?"

"Terex?"

He doesn't reply, and I wonder if I imagined it. Maybe I'm going crazy. But the mishua speeds up, trotting even faster, and I grind my teeth as the pain from my elbow almost makes me cry out.

He's been listening this whole time?

Heat hits my face, and I close my eyes in mortification. Finally, I shrug it off. If my rambling about my trials growing up has managed to give him something to listen to while in that much pain, the least I can do is keep going.

I clear my throat, wondering how much he heard.

"Well, I finally got away for college. I studied my ass off and got a scholarship out of state. By the time I graduated, I knew I wasn't going to be moving back to Louisiana. To be honest, I had no plans to see my family ever again. I know it sounds mean, but you have no idea what it's like being around them. I'm the worst version of myself. I'm small and scared and helpless. I let them bully me, and I let myself believe that what they say is true. My therapist said that it's okay to choose not to be around some people. Even if they're family."

I sigh, realizing I'm justifying it. I haven't met Terex's family, but from what he's told me, they're close. It sounds like his parents are wonderful, and he probably can't imagine choosing to cut himself off from his family.

"Anyway, I hadn't planned to go back, but my mom managed to get in contact. She said she was dying. My friend Tim said if I didn't go and she really *was* dying, I'd regret it for the rest of my life. He's usually right about this kind of stuff."

Terex lets out a low growl, and I jolt in the saddle, cursing when a lightning bolt of pain runs up my arm.

"He's just a friend," I assure him. "We've never even kissed."

Terex growls again.

"Stop it," I snap when he moves his shoulder. "Lie still."

I've managed to wedge more material from my dress beneath his side and where he's draped over the mishua. I'm hoping that the pressure of him lying on the wound will help staunch some of the bleeding.

But what do I know?

"Anyway," I continue. "I went home. Of course, my mother *wasn't* dying, so I'd taken time off work in the middle of the school year and paid for a last-minute flight for no reason."

I scowl, still annoyed.

"Female!"

I look up, blinking my eyes in shock. A warrior stands a hundred feet in front of us, sword in his hand, although he quickly stows it when he meets my eyes.

"Tell me he's a sentry."

Terex doesn't respond. No growls, no groans.

Shit.

We make it to the warrior, and he pales when he sees Terex draped over the mishua.

"I'll ride ahead and get the healers ready. Keep going."

I nod, and Kini speeds up again, likely pleased to be so close to home.

I swallow around the lump in my throat. Terex is no longer responding. I reach out and attempt to feel for a pulse, but we're bouncing so much that my hand slips off his neck.

It feels like time comes in snapshots. I'm suddenly surrounded by warriors, who reach for Terex, faces hard and pale as they take off toward the camp. A warrior I don't know reaches for me, and I jolt back. He simply grabs me in his arms, pulling me onto his saddle, and then we're racing after Terex.

Then, I'm suddenly standing in the healer's kradi, watching all three healers strip off Terex's shirt. The glimmering scales across his shoulders and upper chest look washed-out and faded, and Moni's mouth becomes a thin line as she examines his wound.

She glances at me. "You do not need to be here for this."

"I'm not leaving him."

She sighs but nods, gesturing for me to sit by his side. "Then take his hand, child, and talk to him."

I grab his huge hand and raise it to my lips. I'm suddenly shaking, the aftereffects of the adrenaline hitting me hard. I lean forward, nuzzling Terex's ear.

"You need to be okay," I whisper. "I said I'd kiss you when we got back here, remember? You need to be awake for it though."

Moni does something that makes Terex's brows lower and his body tense. I press a kiss to his cheek, and Moni mutters, her eyes hard as one of the healers hands her a tray of instruments.

I turn my eyes away, feeling queasy, and return to whispering in Terex's ear.

It feels like hours later when Moni finally moves away.

"We have done all we can," she declares, scanning her gaze over Terex's body. "Now it is up to him. Terex is a stubborn warrior. He will choose whether he will go with Death or stay with us."

I nod, shoulders slumping.

"Let me take a look at that elbow, child."

"I'm fine."

"He will not be pleased to see you like this when he wakes up. He will scowl and roar, and it will set his recovery back."

I nod, reluctantly letting Terex's hand go as I move closer to Moni. She's as gentle as can be, her dark eyes sympathetic as she examines my arm.

"What were you thinking?"

I frown at her. "I had to get him on the mishua."

Her eyes widen in surprise, and then understanding sweeps across her face. "You were very brave. This will hurt. But you are learning that sometimes pain is necessary, hmm?"

I nod, my eyes half closed with exhaustion. And then I jerk back as she pulls out her evil green paste, slathering it on my arm. I grind my teeth but refuse to cry out when Terex is in so much more pain. Moni helps me back into the sling, and finally, she lets me curl up next to Terex's warm body, and the healers leave us both alone.

<hr>

Terex

I shake with the cold even as I know I'm burning up.

Fever.

Am I still on the mishua?

Ellie.

I shift, and fire travels up my side as Ellie's sweet scent hits me. She is close by.

My eyes are heavy, and she nuzzles my hair.

"You're okay, Terex. We're back at camp."

A cool cloth wipes my brow, and I shake further.

"C-Cold," I growl, and the cloth pauses.

"You're burning up. I know you're cold, but we need to bring the fever down."

I scowl, and a tiny laugh leaves Ellie's throat. I allow her to do as she wishes. I would allow her anything to hear that sound again.

She managed to get us back to camp. I may still die, but my brave, stubborn female brought me home.

"Terex?"

My father. Ellie stills, and I growl as I feel her move away.

I reach out a hand and catch material. Her dress, perhaps. I pull her close and hear her exasperated snort as I hear my mother let out a choked laugh.

"My son is as stubborn as his father," she says.

I fight to open my eyes, but a vicious headache keeps my lids closed.

I would know my mother's hand anywhere, the skin soft but slightly calloused from a lifetime of work. She runs her fingers over my cheek, and I hear a choked sob.

"I know, he's burning up," Ellie says quickly. "Moni says it's normal and once the fever breaks, he should start to heal. I'm trying to keep him as cool as I can."

I can smell my father, the scent of his favorite leather softener drawing closer. "I heard what happened. Your actions were very brave."

I can almost feel Ellie blush, and I want to smile even as I shiver with fever.

"I did what anyone would've done."

I frown at that, and my mother's hand dances over my brow. "You saved my son's life."

"He saved me first." The words are simple, and I want to drag my tiny female close.

"Rakiz," my mother says suddenly, and I crack open my eyes.

"How's he doing now?" Rakiz asks.

"It's hard to say," Ellie says, her voice trembling. I attempt to turn my head toward her, but my body is weak and useless.

"The fever has taken him," my mother says. A shadow falls over my face, and I manage to meet Rakiz's eyes. It's not often that he looks worried. He's scowling down at me, but relief hits his face when he sees I'm awake.

"You need to get on your feet so I can yell at you," he says, and I attempt to smile, but my eyes immediately slide shut.

Ellie

Terex passes out again, and Rakiz turns to me.

"I would like to speak to you," he says.

I glance back at Terex, but his mom is wiping his face, and she smiles at me, indicating that she'll stay with him.

I don't want to leave, but I force myself to nod and follow Rakiz. He's silent as we walk back toward his huge hut, and I blush as I feel everyone's eyes on me. I'm covered in Terex's blood, and most of the bottom half of my dress is missing, cut away to help staunch Terex's bleeding.

I haven't slept in two days, and I want nothing more than

to curl up next to Terex and go back to sleep.

But no one has told Rakiz what happened, and with Terex so badly injured, that's now my job.

I follow Rakiz into the front room of his hut, and he gestures for me to sit down. Arana offers me some tea, and I take it, blowing on the hot liquid before taking a sip.

I didn't realize how thirsty I was, and I drain the cup. Rakiz waits for me to finish and then gets straight to the point.

"Where are Asroz and Deraz?"

I open my mouth, and we both turn as someone pounds on the door.

Arana opens it, and Asroz stares at me, face pale.

"There they are," I mutter to Rakiz, and he narrows his eyes at me. I can tell Asroz has just arrived back at camp though. He's covered in dust, and his face is pale, likely because he's just heard about Terex.

"Is he alive?"

I nod, getting to my feet. "He's with the healers. His parents are with him."

Rakiz also gets to his feet, staring Asroz in the eye.

"Why don't you tell me why I sent three warriors and only one of them returned, barely alive?"

Asroz swallows but takes a deep breath.

"We decided to split up," he says. "Nerix's camp was just a half day of travel away. Dexar had no information about the Voildi who took the human females, so it made sense to see if Nerix had heard anything."

A muscle ticks in Rakiz's jaw, but he nods. "And what did Dexar say about the other female?"

Asroz's gaze flicks away, and I almost shake my head. He reminds me of one of my kindergarteners, confessing to something they know will get them in trouble. I half expect him to cover his mouth with his hand and mumble at the floor.

"He wasn't cooperative. One of the human females..." Asroz shakes his head, and Rakiz tenses.

"What?" He demands.

"Dexar had information about where the missing female was. He wouldn't tell us until she agreed to stay with their tribe."

Rakiz stares at us for a moment, and then a roar leaves him. We all step back as he pushes open the door of his hut, stalking down the steps toward the mishua pen.

"You probably should have let him know that it was Alexis that stayed," I say.

Asroz's mouth is hanging open, and we all watch as Rakiz calls for his mishua, obviously intent on heading to Dexar's tribe.

Then Nevada and Deraz move out from behind the healer's kradi, and Rakiz freezes, his eyes narrowing on Nevada as if he's a predator and she's his prey.

She's talking to Deraz and completely oblivious to whatever craziness is going on in Rakiz's head. I gasp as Rakiz stalks forward, drags Nevada to him, and plunders her mouth in front of the entire camp.

Everyone freezes, jaws dropping open as he pulls her even closer, framing her face in his hands. Nevada kisses him back, sinking into him until she seems to realize what she's doing, suddenly bringing her hands to his chest and shoving him back.

Rakiz releases her as soon as she struggles, and they stare at each other for one fraught moment.

Then Nevada turns, taking in all the eyes on them, and a dull flush hits her cheekbones. Her hands clench into fists, and she glowers at Rakiz before turning and walking away.

CHAPTER ELEVEN

E *llie*

It's three days before Terex can keep his eyes open for
more than a few moments.

And it's two days after that before he can be moved into
his own kradi.

I took a bath as soon as I could trust that he'd still be
alive when I was finished, and it felt amazing to scrub our
journey—and his blood—from my skin. I changed into a
clean gown, and then I stayed in the healer's kradi, wiping
Terex down with cool water until his fever finally broke.

Now he's scowling at me from his bed, unhappy that I
won't curl up next to him and rest.

"I'm fine, Terex, honestly."

"Do not lie to me, tiny female. You have purple circles
beneath your eyes."

I roll my eyes, and he growls at me. I grin back at him,

just flat-out relieved that he's alive and feeling well enough to be grumpy.

My arm feels good enough that Moni finally let me take it out of the sling. I know I set my healing back, but whatever's in that green paste is magic, and while it's tender, it no longer makes me grind my teeth in pain.

Nevada stopped by earlier. Apparently, the tribe they visited had seen Voildi similar to the pack our warriors described. Now we have some idea of the general region where their territory is located.

"Ellie?" Terex snaps me from my thoughts, and I eye him.

"Yes?"

"I would like to bathe."

"Okay, where should I get the water from?"

He narrows his eyes at me. "Ask one of the servants to fill the bath. Perhaps you can join me, tiny female?"

I nod but ignore that last part. The idea of being naked in a bath with Terex... My face heats, and I scowl as he raises his eyebrow at me.

I know that everyone has their place in this tribe, and the servants are people who choose to do that kind of work, but I grew up in the US of A. Asking a servant to do anything just doesn't come naturally to me.

"I'll be right back."

I wander down to the main meeting area, where Alexis used to hang out. She made friends with a bunch of the other women here, while I spent most of my time with Terex. Now I miss her hilarious jokes and bear hugs. I wish I spent more time hanging out with her when she was here.

"Ellie," one of the women says, and I smile. Seini has brought food to our kradi every day, allowing me to focus on Terex.

"Hi," I say, and she steps forward.

"How's Terex doing?"

"A lot better, actually. He says he wants to bathe."

She grins in relief. Terex is well liked amongst his people.

"That's good news. I'll bring water for a bath."

"Oh, no, that's not what I meant. I can do it."

She raises an eyebrow, and I nod. "Seriously. Just point me toward the water."

Seini nods slowly, but she shows me to the huge fire where women cook and heat water all day. One of them hands me a bucket, and I fill it with warm water. I pause as I realize I can't carry it with both hands. My elbow is a lot better, but Moni warned me that I can't use it to lift anything yet.

I shrug and pick up the bucket with one hand. The handle seems strong enough, and I maneuver the bucket up until it's balancing on one hip, my arm wrapped around it. If I take small steps, it won't spill.

Childbearing hips for the win.

I slowly walk back to Terex's kradi, finding him asleep again when I return. I tiptoe past him and pour the water into the bath.

I return four more times, and by the fifth trip, my back is killing me. Terex is a big guy though, and he'll need a lot of water to cover his body in the bath. Something in my stomach clenches at the thought of him relaxed and naked, and I shake my head.

"He's injured, Ellie. Don't be a perv."

I dump the water in the bath and head straight back to the fire. I'm not paying any attention on my way back to the kradi, so I almost bump into the woman who steps into my path.

She's beautiful. Tall but curvy in all the right places, her low-cut dress highlighting her perky boobs. Her hair is a deep black, and her skin is the light tan I've always wanted but never achieved, no matter how much I tried to bake myself in the sun.

"Hi. Ellie, is it?"

I shift the bucket on my hip, attempting to find a more comfortable spot. "Yep. I don't think we've met?"

"No. My name is Learza. I wanted to say thank you for looking after Terex."

She says his name possessively, as if he's *her* giant warrior, and I blink at her.

"No problem," I mutter and step forward to move around her.

She steps into my way again, and I meet her eyes. Of course, she couldn't have cornered me when my bucket was empty, could she?

"It's just that Terex and I are to be mated," she says, and I feel the blood drain from my face.

"Mated?" I ask through numb lips.

She smiles at me, eyes sparkling. "Yes. I thought I'd die when I heard that he had been so badly injured while trying to protect *you.*"

The barb lands, and I wince. I'll always feel guilty about sitting on the mishua while Terex fought for both our lives.

The thought of the terror I felt makes my voice brittle. "Oh yeah? Then where were you when Terex was in the healer's kradi?"

She blinks at me. "I visited with his parents. I'm like a daughter to them. Soon I *will* be a daughter to them. They convinced me that Terex wouldn't want to see me so upset."

My hands shake, and I feel sick to my stomach.

"Thank you for looking after Terex for me," she smiles,

twisting the knife. "I don't know what I would've done if he hadn't come home to me."

I nod and move on, stumbling over my feet on the way back and spilling water down my dress. By the time I make it back to Terex's kradi, there's more water dripping down my dress than there is left in the bucket.

Terex is awake this time when I return, and his face hardens as he stares at me.

"What," he says dangerously, "do you think you're doing?"

I move past him, blinking back tears. "I'm filling your bath. What does it look like I'm doing?"

"I told you to ask a servant."

"Yeah, well, we don't have servants where I come from." I pour the scant amount of water in the bath and stare down at it, disgusted. The bath isn't even a quarter full.

I shriek as Terex appears in the bathing area.

"What are you doing up? You'll fall!"

He glowers at me, and I blow out a breath as I realize that while his side is obviously hurting him, he's not swaying on his feet.

Turns out giant warriors heal quickly.

And giant warriors are more than a little intimidating when their eyes darken with fury.

I stare back at Terex, and he finally nods, eyes turning cool as he pivots on his feet and strides toward the entrance to the kradi.

"Terex?" I trot after him. "What are you doing?"

Moni hasn't said he's allowed to leave his kradi yet. I slide a glance at his hard face. Somehow, I don't think he cares.

People gasp as Terex stalks toward the water. He's bare-chested, and while his wound has been stitched closed, it's still angry and red, stark against his skin.

"Terex," I hiss, and he ignores me. I blink back tears. He's never been this angry with me before.

Everyone goes silent as he approaches the huge fire.

"Tell me," he says quietly, but no one would mistake his tone for anything less than furious. "Why would you allow the tiny human female to fill my bath when she cannot use one of her arms?"

All eyes immediately turn to me, and more than one face looks unimpressed.

"It's fine," I say even as my face flushes. "I offered, Terex. It's not a big deal."

Terex ignores that.

"This female *saved my life*. She got me back to camp and has run herself into the ground caring for me. And no one thought to help her? You all watched as she struggled? I am ashamed."

I swallow around the lump in my throat, hands shaking at both the reminder of how close Terex came to death and the feel of so many eyes on me.

Seini steps forward. "I should not have allowed Ellie to do this," she says, and her eyes hold sympathy when she glances my way.

"No," I say, glaring at Terex. "You offered to help, and I said I could do it myself. That's on *me*."

Gasps sound, but Terex simply stares at me. Finally, his lips curl in a slow smile. "Oh, I know, tiny female. And we will talk about that later."

My face gets even hotter, and I shake under the eyes of so many people. I'm exhausted, embarrassed, and this giant alien's making it worse!

"You know what?" I say, and it's as if the words come out all on their own. "Fix your own fucking bath."

The crowd collectively inhales, but Terex holds my gaze. Then he throws his head back, roaring with laughter. I stare at him for a moment, stunned by his beauty. His eyes sparkle, his teeth gleam, and I'm sure every other female in the vicinity is thinking the exact same as me.

I don't stick around. I turn and stalk away, too upset and angry to care about what everyone thinks of me. The crowd clears a path as I walk toward Terex's kradi. Suddenly the ground moves, and I shriek as huge hands grab me, throwing me over a hard shoulder.

The movement is easy, as if I weigh nothing, and I'm once again struck by how small I am compared to him.

"Terex? What the hell are you doing?! You're not allowed to lift me!"

One hand comes down on my butt, and I lift my fist to pound it against his back, but I'm too scared that I'll end up opening his stitches.

His laugh is a low rumble, and it sends shivers through me even as I growl in fury.

Within moments, we're at his kradi, and as soon as we're inside, Terex places me on my feet, holding me steady while the blood moves from my head.

"Your stitches," I say, moving my hand to his chest, but he shakes his head.

"I told you, it is fine. Now, how about you explain what you were thinking?"

"You...you..." I'm too mad to talk, and I turn away as Terex sighs.

"Ellie," he starts, and I ignore him, stalking into the bathing area and staring down at the water in the bath.

"Why did you have to embarrass me?" I ask quietly, still refusing to look at him.

Terex growls and steps in front of me. "You have saved my life and cared for me for days even as the shadows beneath your eyes get deeper and darker. You could be forgiven for assuming that it is your duty to look after me. But this is incorrect. It is my duty to look after you. I simply reminded my people that you are my female and should be treated appropriately."

"But I'm not *your* female, Terex!" My voice cracks, and I back away from him. "I just met your fiancée."

"What is this word?"

"The woman who's going to marry you!"

Terex frowns at me. "I do not understand."

"Learza." I stumble over the words, realizing she called it something different. "Mating. You're going to be *mated.*"

Terex's eyes show understanding, and then I gape as the scales on his chest begin changing to a deep, dark purple.

"Learza said this?"

I nod, and he curses as the kradi bells sound.

"We will talk about this," he tells me, stalking back into the sleeping area as I finally let my tears fall.

Terex

I can almost *feel* Ellie's pain, and it makes me want to roar. My people have disappointed me with their actions today. I pause in my pacing. My own actions have also contributed to the sniffling I can hear coming from my tiny female.

I have noted her discomfort with the servants, and yet I told her to ask them to fill the bath. My Ellie is unused to such actions, and I should have known that she would take it upon herself to do the task. She is a stubborn female.

Now she can barely look at me, believing that I have been playing with her while planning to be mated to another woman.

It hurts me that Ellie believes me to be so dishonorable, but I push this thought away for now. Ellie has had a difficult life. She does not yet understand the ways of our people, does not yet believe that I am the one for her.

The kradi bell rings again, pulling me from my thoughts, and I step out to find Arana and Seini waiting. Each hold a large bucket of water, and Seini smiles at me when I gesture for them to enter.

"Thank you," I say roughly. They move toward the bathing area and murmur to Ellie. Her sweet voice sounds, but I am unable to hear what she says.

"We'll be right back," Seini says, and I frown as I focus on her wrist.

"Wait." I stalk back into the bathing area, where Ellie is still staring into the bath as if it holds the secrets to the universe. Her face is wet, and my chest hurts at her pain. I never want to see tears dripping down her beautiful face.

I steel myself against her pain, since she is unlikely to allow me to comfort her while believing I belong to another female.

"Ellie," I say. "Please come with me."

My voice leaves no room for argument, and her eyes spark at me before she sighs, following me back to the fire.

"Seini, please show Ellie your wrist."

Seini holds out her wrist, displaying the gold thread that has been woven in an intricate pattern. This is our most precious material. Once tied around a wrist, it will never fray, never break, never become discolored.

"These are mating bands, tiny female. Once a warrior chooses his female, he asks her to mate with him. If the female finds him worthy, she will claim him in public, wrapping these bands around his wrist."

Ellie's eyes flick to my naked wrists, and I nod at her.

"When the warrior accepts her claim publicly, they have a mating ceremony, and he presents her with her own bands."

I turn to Seini. "Does Learza have any mating bands?"

Seini shakes her head, her eyes kind as she glances at Ellie. "No. And Terex has never asked her to be his mate. I'm sorry if she implied otherwise, Ellie."

Ellie's eyes are filled with tears again, but they soften slightly as they meet mine. She gives Seini a smile, and Seini nods at her before returning for more water.

Ellie retreats back into the bathing room, and I wait, more than willing to be patient until we are completely alone.

Once the bath is ready, I move into the bathing room, where Ellie is pacing back and forth, lost in thought.

"What are you thinking, Ellie?"

She frowns at me but doesn't reply, and I simply raise my eyebrows. Then my hands move to my belt, and I drop my pants to the ground.

CHAPTER TWELVE

E*llie*

I IMMEDIATELY FLICK MY GAZE AWAY, AND TEREX CHUCKLES. I definitely caught a glimpse of his long, hard, mouthwatering...

No, Ellie.

It's not that I don't believe him about Learza. It's just that I'm still coming to terms with exactly how hurt I was at the idea of Terex with another woman. A tall, busty, beautiful woman.

I shouldn't care as much as I do. I shouldn't feel like someone has ripped out my heart and stomped on it after just a couple of weeks on this planet.

We're leaving. As soon as we can get off this planet, we're going back to Earth. And even if the thought of leaving Terex kills me inside, what exactly would I do on Agron?

Like your life was really that great on Earth, Ellie?

The sound of splashing draws me from my thoughts,

and I turn, meeting Terex's amused eyes. He's lounging back in the tub, and I wish desperately for a camera. I want to capture the gleam of candlelight on his skin as the kradi begins to darken, the arch of his eyebrow, the play of his muscles as he leans back, posing invitingly.

He knows exactly what he does to me, and I turn away.

"Ellie?"

"What?"

"This water is warm and clean, and you are tired after caring for me so well. Won't you join me?"

"I'll use the water after you do."

He pauses at that, and then chooses a different approach. "What will it take for you to join me?"

I turn back to him. His expression is crafty as he stares me down. I almost shiver. This is the Terex that negotiates with his king until he gets what he wants.

I shift, barely keeping my eyes on his face. "What do you mean?"

"A bargain, tiny female." His voice is coaxing, dangerous, making me want to rub up against him, and I blow out a breath. He does like his bargains.

"What kind of bargain?" The words are out before I realize I've spoken, and I curse myself for showing my hand.

"I have been invited to a mating ceremony tomorrow. I would prefer to spend my time alone with you, but you might enjoy the experience."

Oh.

Terex knows me well. He knows how curious I am about these people and their culture. He knows I'm too shy and awkward to go by myself. Nevada is unlikely to go—she's too focused on coming up with a plan to get us out of here. And I'm sure as hell not going to go with Vivian.

"Why don't you take me anyway?"

More splashing. I grit my teeth, forcing myself not to look.

"I don't want to. People bother me at these events, hoping to convince me to bring their suggestions and needs to the king. But I could be convinced to give up my alone time with you in exchange for a bath now."

I suppress a smile. The tilt of his head and the slight pout of his lips are ridiculously charming. Suddenly, he reminds me of a little boy trying to negotiate for a later bedtime.

I chew on my lower lip. He's playing me like a violin. The problem is, I *do* want a bath. And I want nothing more than to climb into the warm water with him. At this point, I crave him.

"I won't touch you, tiny female. Unless you ask me to."

I sigh. I only have so much willpower. "Fine. But don't look."

I meet Terex's eyes, and he slowly nods, turning his head away. My hands are shaking as I peel off my dress and drop it on top of his pants, giving the room an intimate feel.

Terex is a gentleman and keeps his eyes averted while I climb in. A muscle pulses in his jaw with the effort not to look, and my heart melts.

"I'm...sorry if I hurt you by accusing you of being with someone else," I say.

His jaw clenches and then relaxes, and he slowly nods, still turned away as I slide into the warm water.

"A warrior's honor is sometimes all he has," he says, and guilt hits me in the gut.

"I apologize. It's just that...Learza is so beautiful."

Terex snorts at that, turning back to me. "She is not the one I want. You are more beautiful than any female I have ever seen before. And you are strong, and brave, and stubborn. I wish you could see yourself the way I see you, my Ellie."

My face heats at that, and I swallow around the lump in my throat. I grasp for something to say, but I've got nothing, so I stay silent, watching the candlelight flicker over Terex's skin.

I wish the bath had bubbles for me to hide beneath, but at least night is falling, and the kradi is now dark enough that Terex won't really be able to see anything unless he chooses to stare into the water.

As usual, though, he's a perfect gentleman. That's one of the things I love about Terex. He's a hardened warrior, used to taking what he wants and demanding obedience. But for me...he's gentle and patient.

"What are you thinking?" His voice is low, and I shiver.

"You said it was your duty to look after me."

I frown as he nods.

"This is true."

"Don't get me wrong, I love how you want to protect me and look after me, Terex. But I want to do the same for you too. Relationships should be an equal partnership."

I feel almost presumptuous referring to whatever we have as a relationship, but Terex tilts his head as he considers what I've said.

"I am a warrior, Ellie. I don't know how much I can change to be like the males you are used to."

I move closer. "I don't want you to change. Never that. I just don't want it to be so one-sided. I want to be able to help you and look after you, just like you want to do the same for me."

He nods slowly. "I will think over what you have said."

I lean back again, but it's like my mouth has a mind of its own. "Why did Learza tell me you were to be mated?"

Terex sighs. "Do you really want to talk about another female while naked and in my bath?"

I stare at him, and he sighs again, but his mouth curls in amusement.

"Perhaps if you moved closer, I would be more inclined to speak of things I do not wish to speak of."

I narrow my eyes at him, and he simply raises his eyebrow. I'm currently sitting at the opposite side of the bath. Terex has his legs on either side of mine, and I've pulled my legs up so I don't accidentally kick him in the nuts.

"I don't want to know that bad."

He smiles at me, and I roll my eyes. Okay, I do want to know. Sue me.

He gestures between his legs, and I give him a filthy look. Terex laughs, and I sigh, my heart fluttering as he grins at me.

"Come sit closer, and I'll tell you *anything* you wish to know."

His voice is pure seduction, and I'm moving before I'm even aware of it. This time, Terex drops his gaze as my breasts rise from the water, and my nipples immediately harden as his attention lands on them.

I blush, but his low groan encourages me when I'd otherwise head for the hills.

I move even closer, and then I freeze as I feel him hard against me.

"Jeez," I blurt. "Are all warriors this big everywhere?"

His brow lowers as he reaches out with one hand, pulling me even closer. "You only need to think about *this* warrior, tiny female."

I roll my eyes at that, and then my eyes slide shut as he

pulls me closer until I'm straddling him, his lips dancing down my neck.

"Your stitches..."

"I'm fine, Ellie. I promise."

I shiver, lost in pleasure as his mouth finally finds mine, and I sigh against him as he takes our kiss deeper, stroking my tongue with his.

Suddenly, I'm needy and desperate, wanting nothing more than the feel of him inside me.

Sensing my urgency, Terex slides his hand to my breast, flicking my nipple. I gasp against his mouth, and he does it again before rolling my nipple between his fingers. My head falls back, and he lets out a low growl, pulling me closer and taking one of my nipples in his mouth. My thighs clench as he flicks with his tongue, driving me crazy as his hand continues to play, tweaking my nipple until it's hard and achy.

I let out a low moan, and this seems to spur Terex on because he pulls his mouth away, kissing me again before murmuring against my mouth.

"Say I can have you, Ellie. Be mine. Please."

I never want to hear this strong warrior beg for anything, but the fact that he's begging for *me*...it feels like a dream. I tried to fight these feelings, and I know deep down that they can only lead to heartache. But I want nothing more than to experience the pleasure I know we'll find in each other's arms.

Life is short. I could've died four or five times since I was taken from Earth. If there's one thing getting abducted by aliens has taught me, it's that you never know when life can change in an instant.

I pull away, staring into Terex's eyes. If I say no, he'll nod, remove himself from the bath, and that will be that.

But I don't want to say no.

I nod, and Terex's eyes widen as if this was the last thing he expected. Then those incredible eyes heat, and my breath blows out in a whoosh as he trails his eyes down my body, his hands moving to cup my butt, pulling me even closer.

"You won't regret giving yourself to me, Ellie."

At this, I blink back tears. Sometimes, it's as if Terex can see into my soul. Like he can see all my insecurities and worries. And he wants me anyway.

I lean forward, nibbling on his lower lip, and he growls against me. One of his hands slides around to my pussy, and I moan as he finds me slick and ready.

"You are perfect," he murmurs against my mouth, and then he pulls back, gazing at me with hunger in his eyes.

My stomach clenches. Never has a man looked at me like this before. I've never been so aware of my body, so needy, so...

His.

I rock against him, gasping as I feel the thick length of him settled so close to where I want him. He hums, flicking my clit, his mouth curling at my gasp. I run my fingers along his scales, and his whole body tenses.

I grin, pleased to find a way to turn him on as much as he does me. "Sensitive, warrior?"

His eyes darken, and if I didn't know—without a doubt —that he'd never hurt me, I'd be worried. Instead, I grin at him, and he leans forward, nipping my lip in retaliation.

My grin widens. For me, sex has mostly been awkward and uncomfortable. It's eye-opening to learn that it can also be fun.

Terex's fingers slide against me, rubbing softly at my clit, and I shudder, writhing against him. He leans down, taking my nipple in his mouth, and rolls it with his tongue as I gasp, his fingers hitting just the right spot.

I shatter in his arms, my mind emptying as my body erupts in pleasure, and I choke out a moan. Terex growls, removing his hand and positioning me against him, his hard cock prodding at my opening.

I tense slightly, more than a little worried about his size.

"Gently, Ellie," he murmurs, and we both groan as I slowly slide down the length of him.

He's huge, filling me up in a way I could never have imagined. He stares at me, then leans forward, claiming my mouth while I sink down on him.

"Mine," he growls against my mouth. "Now you're mine."

I tremble with need, and he positions his huge hands on my butt again, lifting me and then pulling me down as he thrusts into me, making me call out his name.

My mind clears, nothing else existing except Terex and this moment, the pleasure currently overtaking my whole body as Terex moves beneath me.

"Oh God," I groan, and Terex reaches down, flicking my clit just as he thrusts into me again. I fly apart, gasping as he shakes against me, both of us finding release. Another orgasm hits me, rolling over the first, and I slump against Terex, shaken to my core.

Holy shit.

Terex

There is no greater feeling than that of Ellie curled against me.

I stroke one hand along her back, enjoying her soft moan as she snuggles closer. I pull a fur over us, since the fire is dying down. Soon we will not need a fire anymore, and I will take Ellie on long rides and show her all the things I love about this planet.

I know the human females are planning to leave. They assume we don't pay attention when they murmur amongst themselves. Nevada has made it clear that as soon as they find the other females, they will attempt to fix their spaceship so they can find the species they call the Arcav and return to Earth.

The thought makes me want to set the ship on fire. I would never prevent Ellie from leaving me if this is what she truly wants. But I will never be the same if she leaves me. She has been here for such as short time, and already I can't imagine my life without her.

Ellie stretches against me, and I stifle a groan as her soft breasts brush against my chest. I have already taken her many times throughout the night, and her cunt must be sore and swollen by now.

She blinks her eyes open, a smile curling her lips. "Hi."

I grin back, absurdly pleased that I convinced this tiny human to share my kradi. The moment I heard her sweet voice, I knew she would be mine.

Ellie traces the scales on my shoulders. "So you're descended from dragons, huh?"

I nod. This fact seems to interest the human females to no end. It's a source of constant conversation and speculation for them.

I shift, pulling her closer. "You must have evolved on Earth?"

She snorts. "Yeah, but we evolved from primates. That's nowhere near as cool as dragons."

I open my mouth, curious about these primates, but I instantly tense at the sounds of shouting outside.

We both sit up at the commotion.

"You go too far, female!"

"I go just far enough! You may be the boss around here, but you don't give *me* orders."

Ellie stares at me. "Oh shit." She jumps to her feet and moves to the bathing area, quickly pulling on her dress. She throws my pants to me, and we move outside, where a crowd is gathering, many people murmuring in shock.

Our king strides through the camp, his hand wrapped around Nevada's arm. She tugs, and he ignores her, making her trot to keep up with his huge stride.

My mouth drops open as she reaches for her sword, but Rakiz has anticipated this, turning and grabbing her before she can pull it. He traps both of her wrists in one of his hands and marches her through the crowd even as her face turns pale with fury.

"Oh my God." Ellie moves around me and runs after them, and I follow, my stride easily keeping up with her.

Rakiz hauls Nevada into his tashiv, and Ellie flinches as he roars at everyone to leave. She sets her jaw, and I move in front of her, raising my eyebrow as she attempts to dart around me.

"You heard Rakiz."

"He's crazy!"

I send her a look. "Crazier than Nevada?"

She tilts her head at that, the ghost of a smile curling her lips before something hits the wall inside. Her eyes widen as she stares up at me pleadingly, and it takes all my willpower to shake my head.

"Not happening."

I trust my king and do not believe he would ever truly

hurt a female. However, I refuse to allow Ellie to enter such a tense situation.

"What did you think you were doing?" Rakiz roars, and Ellie flinches, staring up at me, wide-eyed.

I lean closer. "He won't hurt her, Ellie. Rakiz is unused to being questioned. Whatever Nevada has done, she must have questioned his authority—"

Nevada laughs, but no one could mistake the sound for amusement. "Exactly what I told you I'd do. We have information about where Charlie is. We have leads about our other friends. And still they're out there, waiting for us to save them. I *told* you I'd go after them if you didn't get the job done."

Ellie sucks in a breath at that and then attempts to knock me aside, almost falling on her ass as she rebounds off me. She narrows her eyes at me as if I pushed her.

"Let me through," she hisses. "Nevada has obviously lost her mind."

Rakiz's voice is colder than I've ever heard it. "And *I told you* that females are not permitted to behave so recklessly in my tribe."

"I'm not a member of your tribe, you giant jackass—"

"Have a care, female."

Another harsh laugh, this time slightly hysterical. "Why do you even give a shit, anyway? This has got nothing to do with you."

I sigh. That is the wrong approach to take. These human females do not seem to understand that it is a warrior's birthright to protect those under their care—and none take this more seriously than our king.

"Enough," Rakiz says, voice hard. "You stole food and weapons and attempted to leave this camp after I forbade such a thing. For this, you will be punished."

"Punished?" Nevada's voice is high and incredulous, and I snort at her outrage. Ellie glowers at me, and I hide a smile.

"Be thankful, female, that I am not taking you over my knee the way you richly deserve," Rakiz says.

"Be thankful I haven't decided to cut off your balls and shove them down your throat."

Rakiz's face is hard as stone, but he chooses to ignore that comment. I nod. His control is legendary.

"You want to dress like a male and fight like a male? Fine. You can also work like a male. You will work with the mishua until I believe you have learned your lesson."

Ellie stares at me, and I barely hide my shock. To give a female such labor? With the mishua?

Nevada snorts. "You don't know it yet, but you're going to regret this decision," she promises.

Perhaps Rakiz is right. This female seems unable to learn her lessons.

The door flies open, and Nevada's eyes widen as she sees us. Ellie moves forward, and I allow it, watching as she pulls Nevada into a hug.

"You didn't tell me you were leaving," Ellie murmurs.

"I didn't want you to get into trouble if you knew. You're the worst at keeping secrets. Your face tells everyone what you're thinking."

Ellie smiles, but it quickly falls from her face. "The mishua?"

Nevada snorts. "He's going to have to do better than that." She slides me a look, and I raise an eyebrow. "These warriors seem to think women were designed for them to boss around. But he'll learn. You want to put a tiger on a leash? Don't be surprised when it rips your fucking face off."

With that, Nevada casts one last filthy look at the tashiv and then stalks off, a scowl on her face.

I meet Rakiz's eyes as he appears in the doorway.

"What is a tiger?" he asks Ellie, and while his voice and posture are once again calm, I know him well enough to see the fury still lingering in his eyes.

"Um, it's a giant cat. Jeez, you guys probably don't have them either, huh? It's a four-legged wild animal with fur and sharp claws and teeth."

Rakiz nods, and the last of the fury gradually drains from his eyes as he stares after Nevada.

"They sound like a karja," he says, and I smile at the reference.

Karja are wild beasts, dangerous and fierce. But very rarely, they have been known to be tamed by incredibly patient warriors.

And Rakiz is nothing if not patient.

CHAPTER THIRTEEN

E *llie*

I SMOOTH MY DRESS WITH MY HANDS, PLEASED AT THE WAY IT
falls. Apparently, Terex arranged for this dress to be made
days ago. He was always going to take me to the mating ceremony, and when I pointed this out, he simply shrugged and
said he'd rather see me wear it in his kradi.

It's beautiful, a dark purple material that has a soft
sheen to it. It's cut lower than any of the other dresses I've
worn here, and Arana also sent along an undergarment that
ties under my breasts and over my shoulders—the Braxian
version of a bra, I guess.

Whatever it is, it pushes my boobs up to new heights,
and I'm nibbling my lip, wondering if it's too much when
Terex walks in.

His eyes darken appreciatively as he scans my body.

"Ellie," he says, voice hoarse. "You could not be more
beautiful."

I grin at him even as my cheeks heat. As much as I find his compliments difficult to believe, there's no faking his reaction. His erection is tenting his pants, and he prowls toward me, jaw tight as he pulls me against him.

"We do not need to go to the mating ceremony," he murmurs in my ear before nibbling his way down my neck. "Perhaps we can stay here instead..."

My laugh becomes a groan, and I shiver as he finds a particularly sensitive spot. Terex immediately returns his attention to that spot, running his teeth beneath my ear until I groan again.

I sink against him, instantly wet and ready, but I can hear music starting somewhere in the distance. Not to mention, my vajajay isn't used to so much attention. Terex has taken me too many times to count since our bath, and I'm worried that if I don't give it a rest for a few hours, my pussy will end up as chafed as my thighs were when I first arrived.

I push away, placing my hand over Terex's mouth. He immediately kisses my palm, and my willpower flees.

No, Ellie. Keep your head in the game.

"I want to go," I say. "We can continue this...later."

Terex's eyes darken further, but he nods, and I remove my hand as he smiles down at me.

"You make me happy, Ellie," he says, and my heart melts.

"You make me happy too," I murmur, and satisfaction gleams in those incredible eyes.

"Let's go to the ceremony now so you can see the mating and then return to my furs where you belong."

I laugh but allow Terex to lead me out of the kradi and through the camp to the huge communal area. Behind the massive fire and cooking kradi is a grass meadow, where long tables and stools have been set up in a semicircle. Kids are running around, laughing as they play a Braxian version of tag while adults greet the happy couple.

They're standing together, holding hands, and happiness radiates from them as they smile and laugh with those who bring them gifts.

"Oh no, were we supposed to bring something?"

Terex glances at me and then smiles as his attention turns back to the couple.

"I have already gifted Jarix with a sword befitting his status." He nods at where the sword rests on the warrior's hip, and Jarix seems to feel his attention, looking up at us and grinning.

"What about his...mate?"

"My mother made Rani's dress."

"Wow."

It's beautiful, hugging her body in all the right places while still remaining elegant. The deep-blue outer layer is cut strategically, revealing a shimmery green layer underneath. I wonder how these people create such bold colors, and I open my mouth to ask and then snap it closed as another thought occurs to me.

"Terex," I hiss. "Did your mom make my dress?"

He glances at me and nods, frowning as I gape at him.

"You didn't think to tell me that? Oh my God, I haven't even thanked her!"

I search frantically in the crowd, but I can't pick out his mom with so many people around.

"Relax, Ellie. My mother is a renowned dressmaker. Other tribes bargain with us for the chance to trade for her clothes."

I narrow my eyes at him. "That makes it even worse."

He raises an eyebrow, and I turn, still searching the

crowd. Males. Whether five years old or fifty, human or alien warriors, they're all the same.

Terex seems amused with my reaction, his lip curling. "Come, tiny female. I'll introduce you to Rani and Jarix. Then we can find my mother."

I nod, and we make our way through the crowd. With so many people here, it's easy to see how few women the tribe has compared to men.

I keep an eye out for Nevada, but she's nowhere to be seen. I spot Vivian sitting at a table near the back, and she nods at me. I smile, surprised.

Many of the women eye me as I pass, their gazes flicking to Terex, where they linger appreciatively. I find myself shooting them dirty looks, and I'm so distracted that I barely notice when we arrive in front of the mated couple.

"It's so nice to meet you," I say to Rani while Jarix and Terex grab each other's forearms in greeting.

"You too," she says, staring at me. There's no disdain in her gaze, just simple curiosity, but I find myself shifting awkwardly under her regard anyway.

"I heard that you enjoy children," she says, and I glance at Terex, but he's still talking to Jarix.

"I do." I smile. "On Earth, it's my job to teach them."

Rani smiles back at me. "In this tribe, I spend most of my time with the youngest children, teaching them numbers. Would you like to join me one day soon?"

My heart clenches, and I'm nodding my head before I even realize I'm doing it. I miss my kids something fierce. While teaching is hard, underpaid work, for me, it was the most rewarding job I could imagine.

Terex and Jarix wrap up their conversation, and Terex takes my hand, pulling me close to one of the tables. I meet his mom's eyes, and she smiles at me from where she's sitting with Terex's dad.

"I just realized I have no idea what your parents' names are," I murmur, breaking out in a cold sweat. If I thought I suffered from social anxiety on Earth, I had no idea what was in store for me on Agron. For reasons I can't explain, I desperately want Terex's parents to like me.

"My mother's name is Kara, and my father's name is Corva."

I nod, pasting a smile on my face as we arrive at the table and they gesture for us to join them.

"Kara," I begin as soon as the pleasantries are finished, "thank you so much for the dress. It's gorgeous."

She runs her gaze over my body, giving me a pleased nod. "It looks lovely on you. Thank *you* for looking after my son. He wouldn't have been happy to have his mother at his side for every moment of his recovery."

I glance at Terex from under my lashes, and his hand moves to my thigh under the table as I hold back a smirk at the thought of his "recovery," most of which he spent attempting to coax me into his bed.

He shoots me a wicked grin, and I immediately dart my gaze away, refusing to let him make me blush in front of his parents.

Corva gives me a knowing look, opening his mouth just as Rakiz appears.

"Terex," he says, nodding at the table in greeting. "We are ready."

Terex gets to his feet, and Kara leans over, patting my hand. "Terex is often called to officiate these types of things. He is a warrior like no other," she says, and Corva nods proudly.

"It's good luck to have a strong warrior preside over a

mating." She glances at me. "My son is a fearless warrior," she continues, and I tilt my head but nod. "It is past time that he took a mate."

I see where this is going. I open my mouth as Kara smiles at me. "You have been good for Terex," she says. "He has been different since he found you, smiling more easily. You fit in well with our tribe."

Well.

I wouldn't quite agree with that, but a bell sounds, and I turn my attention back to the ceremony.

We all watch as Terex moves toward the couple. A fire has been started while we were talking, and it's burning bright, the flames throwing off enough heat that sweat begins to gleam on Terex's chest as he and Jarix both remove their shirts.

I glance at Kara, and she smiles, gesturing for me to watch.

The warriors stand on either side of the fire, about ten feet back on each side. Rani is lit from within as she beams, moving toward Terex.

The crowd goes silent as Terex lifts Rani in his arms, waiting while she arranges her dress. She pulls it into her lap so that the beautiful material doesn't hang down.

Then suddenly, without warning, Terex throws Rani high over the fire. I jump to my feet, but Jarix grins, jumps forward, and leaps over the fire, catching his mate in his arms.

Neither of them truly came close to the fire, but my heart is pounding like a drum anyway. Corva grins at me.

"The fire symbolizes purity, new life, and passion. Rani has put her trust in Jarix, and with his actions, he states that he will always catch her if she falls."

I swallow around the lump in my throat and nod. Truthfully, it scared the shit out of me but only because I wasn't expecting it. In my mind, I'm replacing Rani with myself, and Terex's strong arms are catching me.

I shake off the thought, returning my attention to the ceremony. Jarix rolls up his sleeves, revealing gold bands similar to the ones Seini showed me. An older man steps forward, placing two more bands in his hands, and I blink back tears, realizing he's Jarix's dad.

God, I miss my dad.

It took me years to make it through a whole day without crying once he was gone. Now I can almost see it as a blessing that he's not around to learn about what happened to me. If he'd woken up one day and found me missing, he would've spent the rest of his life trying to find me.

Terex meets my eyes across the meadow, and I give him a shaky smile. My dad would've loved him. He was a man of few words, but he respected strength and honor.

Jarix steps forward, his eyes hot as he gazes at Rani. "My love," he says. "I have made these bands to represent our bond. Strong, true, and never to be broken. Will you accept them?"

Rani nods, a tear rolling down her cheek. "I will."

Jarix ties one of the gold bands around each of her wrists.

Cheers sound, and Rakiz steps forward. Rani turns to him, and the crowd goes silent as the king takes her hands, kissing the skin beneath each of her golden bands.

"May your mating be blessed for all days."

Rani smiles at him, nodding her head, and then Rakiz places her hand in Jarix's.

Jarix grins, nodding at Rakiz. Then Jarix pulls Rani to him, taking her mouth in a deep kiss, and the crowd goes wild, jumping to their feet and clapping. Cheers sound, and I brush tears off my face.

The ceremony was short, completely different to anything I've seen on Earth, and incredibly beautiful.

***

Terex

"Mmmm..."

I grin, pausing to look up at my tiny female, and her brow creases as I stop. She moves languidly, her hips twisting as she searches for the pleasure I give her.

The pleasure that only I will ever give her.

I push her thighs further apart, and her eyes flutter open, still glazed with sleep and heavy with lust. I groan at the sight, and she gasps as I bury my face between her soft thighs, licking and nibbling at her sweet cunt.

"Terex," she moans, and triumph fills me. I lave her clit, and she writhes, her hands moving to my hair, holding me tight against her.

The feel of her hands guiding me for her pleasure, the sound of her soft moans, the taste of her cunt...

It takes every ounce of my self-control to not embarrass myself. I blow out a breath and attempt to think of something else even as I gently suck her clit, applying the tiniest pressure with my teeth.

"Oh my God." Ellie lifts her head, eyes wide, and then she chokes out a strangled moan as I push two fingers inside her, curling them to hit the spot that makes her wild.

At this, she comes with a loud groan, and I grin, pleased that any warriors nearby will know my female has been claimed.

Her eyes are dazed, sliding closed as she trembles, and I growl at the sight. I have to have her. Now.

I flip her onto her stomach, and she pushes up her plump ass, the sight better than I could ever have imagined. My cock is so hard it's painful, and I position it at her slick entrance, almost losing control as I ease into her.

"Terex," Ellie groans, her hands scrabbling to clutch at the fur. "Take me."

There is no greater pleasure than the feel of Ellie beneath me. No greater sound than her voice begging me to make her mine.

She may be wet, but she's still tight, and a sweat breaks out on my body as I strain for control, slowly inching forward.

Ellie sighs, and then I'm growling, shaking as she thrusts back into me, and I slide all the way in.

Where I belong.

I withdraw, slamming back inside her, her continual groans encouraging me. I feel as if it'll never be enough. I'll never be deep enough inside her, not until she admits she's mine.

Ellie raises her hips, and I slide one hand underneath her breasts, rolling her nipples as she gasps. I move my fingers down to the place where our bodies meet, and her cunt clenches on me as I brush my fingers over her clit.

"Oh God, Terex, yes..."

I play with her clit again, needing her to come before I lose all control.

"Come for me, Ellie," I growl, and I squeeze my eyes shut, gasping out a curse as she does, her whole body shuddering as her cunt pulses, and my body responds, pleasure shooting from my balls up my spine and back down again as

I release into her, finally slumping, careful not to crush her with my weight.

"Mmm," she murmurs, eyes drifting closed. "What a way to wake up."

I laugh, slowly pulling out of her and finding a cloth to clean her thighs. She opens her eyes, cheeks heating, and I grin at her shyness.

"I must go soon, tiny female," I say, my grin widening at her adorable pout. "I promised Rakiz I would attend his meeting with the council."

I frown at the thought, wanting nothing more than to spend the day here, in the furs with Ellie.

"That's okay." She yawns sleepily. "I think I'll go see Nevada. I haven't seen her for a couple of days."

I nod, lips curling. Rakiz has his hands full with that one. I pull Ellie closer. The council members will still be stepping over each other, fighting for the seats closest to their king.

"What else will you do today?" I lean close, breathing in the scent of Ellie's hair.

"I thought I'd go talk to Rani. She mentioned something about helping out with the kids."

I nod, my good mood dampening slightly. Ellie said she *is* a teacher on Earth, as if that is still her life. I didn't miss the longing in her eyes even as she turned to smile at me.

I frown, and Ellie reaches up, running her hand over my brow.

"What's wrong?"

"Nothing. I'm glad you're going to spend time with the children. I can tell you love them."

She smiles up at me. "I do. I always knew I wanted to be a teacher. My childhood kind of sucked a lot of the time, you know? But a few of my teachers really stood out. When I was being bullied in high school, Mrs. Avery sat me down. She told me that if I wanted a ticket out of that town, the answer was to get good enough grades to get a scholarship. Otherwise, she said, I'd be stuck in the same town with the people who made my life miserable, only we'd be adults. Then she did everything she could to help me throughout the rest of my time at school."

"A scholarship?"

"Yeah. I applied for schools I knew that no one from my high school was applying for. I didn't care where the colleges were, only that they were far enough that I couldn't come home very often, and I wouldn't run into any of the people who were so mean to me."

I frown. "I do not like the thought of you running from your home."

Ellie pulls back from me, her expression wounded. "I wasn't running away. I was..." Her voice trails off. "I guess I *was* running away. But you would too. I guess *you* wouldn't, since you're *you*."

She stares into the distance, and I sit up.

"I didn't mean it that way, Ellie. I only meant that I don't like that you were forced to leave. If I had known you, I would have protected you."

Her expression clears, and she grins at me. "I'd love to have seen you stalking down the corridors at my school. Although, you'd probably have dated my sister..."

"Never," I tell her. "I would only have had eyes for you."

She gives me a smile like she doesn't quite believe me, and I pick up her hand, nibbling at her fingers.

"You don't yet understand, tiny female, but you will." With that, I roll away from the temptation of Ellie's body and reach for my pants.

CHAPTER FOURTEEN

E*llie*

"Wow, it stinks."

I gag a little, moving a few steps to the side to inhale some fresh air.

Nevada turns, a strangely shaped shovel in her hand. "Yeah, no shit."

We both grin as we stare at the mountain of Mishua poop she's creating.

"How are you?"

"Better than you'd think." Nevada wipes the back of her hand across her forehead, leaving a brown smear that I really hope is dirt. She catches my expression, and her nose wrinkles as we both stare at each other, revolted, and then burst out laughing.

"God, who would've thought that this would be how I'd end up on an alien planet?" she says finally. She moves to wipe her eyes, and I step forward.

"Ew. No. Let me."

I wipe under her face with the sleeve from my dress, and her bright-green eyes laugh at me before she sobers, leaning on her shovel.

"How was the mating ceremony?"

"It was good. I wish you'd come."

She shrugs. "I had things to do."

"What kind of things?"

Nevada sends me a look and then shrugs again. "I'm going after Beth, Ivy, and Zoey. I've been shamelessly eavesdropping and collecting information, and after our visit to the Krazion tribe, I've got a pretty good idea of where they would've been taken."

I chew on my lower lip, anxiety hitting me hard. "It's so dangerous, Nevada."

She nods. "I know." Her voice gentles. "I'm not an idiot, Ellie. I know it's not the best idea I've ever had. But here's the thing. I've got food, clean water, clothes, and somewhere to sleep. No one's planning to eat me or sell me, or anything else. We can't say the same for the other women. I can't just sit around here and do nothing."

Guilt hits me hard. That's exactly what I'm doing. "I'll come with you."

She immediately shakes her head. "You've done enough. It's 'cause of you that we have the information we do. And no offense, Ellie, but you're useless in a fight."

Fair call. I blow out a breath. "What if I convinced Terex to help? We could all go."

"Don't say a word to him," Nevada says, voice serious. "He'll tell Rakiz, and then I won't be going anywhere. You know that asshole is making me sleep in his hut? He decided he wants to keep an eye on me. I'm still deciding whether to take a bath after I'm finished here. As much as

I'm dreaming of clean water, I'd love to stink up his place."

I smirk. "You're both as bad as each other."

She laughs and then sobers again. "Look, Ellie, I'm experienced in the outdoors. Okay, this planet's different, but the basic rules apply." She blows out a breath and glances around before leaning close. "Right before the Arcav invaded, I was a prisoner of war in Baghdad. The only thing that got me through was knowing that someone would be coming for me. They weren't going to leave me behind."

She blinks, looking away, and I nod firmly.

"Are you seriously going to leave me with Vivian?"

She laughs. "She's not that bad. Honestly, I feel sorry for her."

I scoff, thinking of Vivian's perfect face. "Yeah, her life must be so hard."

Nevada tilts her head, eyes serious. "Vivian has obviously been taught that her only worth is connected to how she looks. You and I know better. And on this planet, her looks will only get her so far. We're all aliens here." She grins at me. "Now are you with me?"

I blow out a breath. "Fine. How can I help?"

- - -

Terex

Ellie is quiet and withdrawn this morning, smiling absently at me while she gets dressed.

"Is everything okay?"

She nods, standing on tiptoe, and I lean down so she can kiss me. Just like that, I want her again, and she laughs as I pull her close.

"Terex, I have to go. I told Rani I'd help her with the kids today."

I smile at the thought. My Ellie loves children. I watched her play with them at the mating ceremony, and since she arrived at our camp, the little ones have been quick to run to her, calling her name when she is walking through the camp. She always crouches down to their level, nodding at their stories and promising to play with them.

"Fine. But don't let Harix kiss you again," I mock growl, and she laughs. Harix is just four summers old and can often be found trailing Ellie throughout the camp.

I freeze as someone approaches, footsteps pounding on the ground, and within moments I've pushed Ellie behind me, drawing my sword as she gasps.

Rakiz strides into our kradi, face hard with rage. "Where is she?" he roars, and Ellie flinches, paling.

I step forward. "Rakiz, what is this?"

He ignores me. "Tell me, female," he says softly, and Ellie's lips firm mutinously.

He steps closer, and I throw my sword to the ground but step in front of Ellie.

"Watch yourself, Rakiz," I say. He may be my king, but this is my territory and *my* female who is trembling.

"The hellion has disappeared," Rakiz says, his gaze cold as it finds mine. "I don't believe she acted alone."

I turn to Ellie. "Is this true?"

"I—"

"Where did she go?" Rakiz growls impatiently.

"Where do you think?" Ellie's voice shakes, but she stares Rakiz down. "She went looking for our friends."

Rakiz lets out a vicious oath. "*Where?*"

"I don't know. She's been listening in and making plans. She figured out where they're most likely to be taken."

Rakiz glances at me, and I almost reach for my sword at the threat in his eyes.

"She took my mishua."

I tense, stunned. Surely the female would not be so stupid. Ellie sighs, covering her face with her hand. This part of Nevada's plan, at least, she didn't know.

Mishua are extremely dangerous, but none more so than the king's.

"How could she have taken it?"

Rakiz grinds his teeth. "I had her working in the mishua pen. She likely took the opportunity to build some sort of relationship with the beast."

Ellie clears her throat. "If the mishua let her ride it, it can't be that dangerous, right?"

Rakiz turns away, and I sigh. I don't know what exactly he feels for Nevada, but regardless, he considered her under his protection. Now...

"The mishua may allow her to ride it one moment and then kill her the next," I say. "The king's mishua is highly intelligent and easily bored. It may allow Nevada on its back purely for the chance to return to the wild."

Ellie's face drains of color, and I glance away, ruthlessly suppressing any sympathy. For her to keep this from me...

"I will find her," Rakiz snarls, and I nod. More of our warriors returned last night, so he will be able to send them after Nevada.

Rakiz stalks from the kradi, and I turn my attention back to Ellie, who has tears dripping down her face.

"Are you so desperate to return to your planet that you would risk your friend's life?"

She blinks at me, and I curse, turning away at the hurt in her eyes.

"It's not like that, Terex."

"It's not? Why would you not tell me of this?"

"I promised Nevada. You would have had to tell Rakiz. You know you would have."

"To save her life!" I roar, turning back to Ellie. "She has no idea about the dangers on this planet—"

"Of course she doesn't," Ellie snaps, hands fisting at her sides. "Because you guys refuse to tell us anything. How would you feel, Terex, if it was the other way around? If you landed on Earth and your friends were missing, but we just patted you on the head and told you we'd take care of it? On our planet, Nevada's a warrior—just like you are here. Rakiz could have worked *with* her, but he forced her hand."

I gape at her, and then a growl leaves my throat. "Females are to be protected."

She tilts her head with a sigh, opening her mouth, and I hold up a hand.

"I cannot speak of this right now," I say, stalking from the kradi.

Ellie

Stunned, I blink back tears as Terex leaves. That was our first real fight, and my stomach roils uneasily as I blow out a shaky breath.

I can see his point of view, but I don't understand why he can't see mine. Sure, I wish I could've told him what Nevada was planning. But he would've told Rakiz, and the king's reaction demonstrated exactly how that would've gone down.

Unfortunately, with so few females in this tribe, these warriors seem to think that we should be coddled and protected. Me? I love the idea of Terex keeping me safe. But that doesn't mean that Nevada wants the same thing.

I wipe away tears, cursing as I pull on the boots Terex had made for me. He's so thoughtful, and the look in his eyes when he asked if I was desperate to leave him…

Don't think about it now, Ellie. He'll calm down.

I blow my nose, heading out of the kradi and toward the large clearing where the mating ceremony was performed. Apparently, the kids get to learn outside on warm days—something that my kindergarteners would have loved.

I spend the morning playing with the kids, teaching them to count using colorful rocks and different-sized sticks, which are more often than not used for mock sword fights.

Chani has taken a liking to me. I'm assuming she's about six or seven, but she could be younger, since Braxian kids are so much bigger than human kids. I'm sitting on a log in the sun braiding her hair when Jarix arrives, murmuring to Rani. Her eyes widen in shock, and she glances at me.

"Go play, darling," I say to Chani, and she smiles, jumping off my lap and taking one of the larger sticks.

"I'm going to be a warrior like Nevada," she announces, snarling at the boys when they laugh at her.

I get to my feet, and Rani meets me, her face pale.

"What is it?"

"Rakiz has left the tribe."

"What?"

She nods. "He told no one where he was going, but it is likely he has followed your friend."

There's a hint of condemnation in her eyes, and I bristle.

"He wouldn't allow Nevada to find our friends," I say. "They're women, just like us, scared and alone on an alien planet."

She nods. "But Nevada is just a female."

I scowl at that. "She's tough and strong, and she knows what she's doing. It was her choice."

"And now our tribe is without our king," Rani says softly, and I flinch.

"I'm sorry," I say. "I think I should go."

"Ellie—"

My hands are shaking as I walk back toward our kradi. I'm tired. Bone tired.

Vivian appears on the path in front of me, her face white. I glance behind me, but her eyes narrow on me. Awesome.

"Why didn't you tell me Nevada was leaving?"

I frown at her. "She asked me not to tell anyone."

"Why didn't she tell me?"

"I don't know, Vivian, maybe because she thought you wouldn't care?"

Her face flushes, and for a moment I feel bad.

"I'm sorry," I say, but she backs away, eyes hard.

"Not all of us have a giant warrior to help us escape our reality," she says. "Nevada was my only friend here, and now she's probably going to die because you let her go off alone."

"You think I don't wish I'd managed to talk her out of it? You're not the only one who cares about her, Vivian. And if she dies, I'm the one who'll have to live with the guilt."

Her mouth opens, but I'm not done, and I hold up a hand. "And you know what? You could've had another friend here too, but you were too busy trying to make me feel like shit."

Vivian turns and stalks away, brushing at her face, and guilt hits me. Again. I should've tried harder to convince Nevada not to go. Maybe I should've told her to talk to Rakiz one more time, or at least talk about her plan with Vivian.

I walk into the kradi, wanting nothing more than to curl up under the furs with Terex.

Unfortunately, Learza has beaten me there.

She's standing close to Terex, her voice low and intimate. Terex is scowling, obviously still in a bad mood, but as I watch, she says something that makes him smile, following it up with a comment that makes him throw his head back, roaring with laughter.

The way he only does with me.

My throat itches, and I swallow, my hands shaking as Learza reaches her hand up, wiping something off his forehead.

Terex allows it, smiling down at her, and then he turns, his eyes narrowing on my face as he sees me standing there. He moves toward me, but I turn, vision blurring as I stumble away.

He didn't do anything, Ellie. Get your shit together. Just because she looks like a taller, curvier Victoria's Secret model doesn't mean he wants to bang her like a drum.

My mantra doesn't help. I just need to be alone for a while. Surely there's a spot somewhere where I can sit and think about my life choices.

There's a small stream behind Rakiz's hut. I move through the camp as if I'm sleepwalking, and my shoulders slump in relief as I find the spot empty. I sit on a huge rock and stare at the water.

"Ellie."

"I need some time alone, Terex."

A low growl, followed by a curse. "What are you thinking?"

I turn my head, meeting his eyes, *hating* that he's so attractive, that so many women want him. How long will it be before he realizes his mistake and finds someone else?

How much more could I fall for him in that time? And could I survive losing my home *and* Terex?

"I'm thinking that whatever we're doing could be a mistake," I say and instantly want to take it back as his face hardens, a wounded look in his eyes.

"Why would you say such a thing?"

"What were you doing with Learza, Terex?"

Confusion crosses his face. "Speaking with a friend."

"Have you slept with her?"

His eyes narrow. "Yes. Many years ago."

I let out a choked laugh, and he stalks closer.

"When have I given you reason to doubt my honor?"

"You haven't—"

"What do I have to do to prove to you that I'm yours?"

"Terex—"

He waves his hand, cutting me off, and my heart twists in my chest as his eyes turn cold.

"You've never once said the same to me. You will still leave me if you can, won't you? You'll get in your ship and fly back to your home planet where males are not warriors and do not take what they want. And you'll never see me again. Will you even think of me, Ellie?"

Will I think of him? He has to be kidding, right? All I think about is him.

When I don't reply, too stunned to know what to say, he lets out a harsh laugh.

"Perhaps you are right," he says, his voice colder than I've ever heard it. "Perhaps this *was* a mistake. For both of us."

"Wait, Terex—" I open my mouth, but I still don't have the words. He stares at me for one moment and then shakes his head, leaving me alone.

The way I thought I wanted to be.

CHAPTER FIFTEEN

E*llie*

I SIT BY THE STREAM AS A LIGHT DRIZZLE BEGINS TO FALL, thinking longingly of a hot shower. How many times did I used to think nothing of stripping off my clothes, turning on the water, and standing in the shower until I thawed after my long commute in winter?

I took it for granted, the way we humans seem to take most things for granted.

We get home after a long day, throw our clothes in the washing machine, take a shower, and turn on the TV without a thought. It's not until we're abducted by aliens—or suffer some other calamity—that we appreciate those modern conveniences.

I sigh. When I'm with Terex, I never think about the stuff I miss from home. Oh, sure, I'd love to be able to plug in my hair dryer occasionally, but who needs a blast of hot air when you've got an alien warrior who loves brushing your hair by the fire?

I sniff, blinking back tears. At least, he used to love it. Until I ruined it with my jealousy and insecurity.

What's wrong with me?

"Ellie?"

I keep my eyes on the stream. "What is it, Vivian?"

"I wanted to apologize."

I'm glad she can't see my expression right now. She'd probably turn right around and leave at the shock on my face.

"Apologize?"

She sighs. "Yeah. Look, I know we haven't been close, and some of that's my fault. I shouldn't have yelled at you earlier. No one can argue with Nevada when she's made up her mind."

I smile, swallowing around the lump in my throat. She's right, of course. Right now, I miss Nevada like a limb.

"It's okay, Vivian, I get it."

Her voice hardens. "You could at least look at me, you know."

I blow out a breath as I turn, wiping the tears from my face, and Vivian narrows her eyes at me.

"What's wrong?"

I sniff. "Nothing."

She raises her eyebrow. "Does it have anything to do with your warrior storming through the camp like he wants to kill something?"

Tears fill my eyes again, and she raises her eyebrow.

"You had a fight?"

"We broke up. At least, I think we did. I mean, I don't know if we were ever truly an actual couple..."

"Not a couple? Could've fooled me. Why'd you

break up?"

I sigh. For once, Vivian's not being a total bitch, and let's face it: there's no one else here to talk to.

"I was feeling insecure about all the women throwing themselves at him. He got pissed about it, we argued, and he basically told me he's sick of having to prove himself to me. Oh, and that he knows I'm going to forget about him when I go home anyway."

I brush more tears off my face and Vivian narrows her eyes at me.

"Do you want to stay here?"

"I don't know… We've never actually had that conversation, you know? Even a few days ago, I would've said no, but when he brought it up like that… It just really hit me that I'd truly never see him again."

She shakes her head, and for a moment, sympathy sparks in her eyes, but it's quickly replaced by annoyance. "You know what your problem is?"

I sigh. Here we go. "What?"

"You don't know what you want, and when you do, you're too scared to fight for it. I don't blame the big guy. He's done everything except tattoo his name across your forehead to prove you're his, and you won't fight for him at all. These warriors are savages. They're used to taking what they want. Meanwhile, you refuse to take control of your life."

Ouch. Did I say Vivian's not in bitch mode? I take it back. To be fair, Nevada would probably give me the same real talk.

"We're leaving," I say.

She shrugs. "Then I guess you shouldn't care if you're no longer together." She tilts her head as if contemplating something. "Maybe Terex will be looking for a roll with someone else since you don't want him."

I bare my teeth at her, fury hitting me hard, and she widens her eyes slightly and then grins before turning and strutting away with a flick of her hair.

Terex

Ellie hasn't returned to our kradi. Her dresses are still here, her hairbrush on my table, but she's nowhere to be found.

Can I blame her?

I think over my angry words and sigh. My tiny female looked wounded, her face draining of color. But still, she didn't deny her plans to leave.

I curse, striding back and forth. My kradi feels empty without Ellie, and I want nothing more than to find her and haul her back to where she belongs.

But what will change? She'll still believe that I want other females, even when I've reassured her time and time again that I want no one but her.

I scowl at my furs, where Ellie should be lying, a smile on her beautiful face while she waits for me to join her.

I'm the worst version of myself. I'm small and scared and helpless. I let them bully me, and I let myself believe that what they say is true.

Ellie's voice runs through my head, and I stare into the fire. A thread of sorrow ran through her words—words she only spoke in an attempt to keep me conscious.

It worked. Stories of her childhood gave me something to cling to when I could feel my blood soaking into my clothes. Still, I didn't truly understand how those around her had made her believe she was inferior until today.

It's clear that Ellie will never claim me the way I want to claim her. She'll never believe I truly want *her*. Now instead of talking to her, attempting to understand, I've driven her away.

She'll go back to her planet and find *Tim*. I snarl and get to my feet, pacing back and forth. I'll find Ellie. I'll bring her back and make her see—

No.

I grit my teeth, every muscle in my body aching to find my tiny female and convince her that she's mine. But if she can't believe such a thing, can't believe in *me*...I don't know where that leaves us.

***

Ellie

I move into Vivian's kradi, curling up in the bed Alexis used when she was still here. Vivian pauses when she enters, likely staring at my still form while I sniffle, the warm furs over my head.

I can practically *feel* her roll her eyes.

"If you're going to stay in here, you need to quit crying. You're messing with my chi."

I pull the blanket down slightly and glower at her, and the hint of a smile appears on her lips.

"Fine," she says. "But at least eat something. Your warrior will lose his mind if you become skin and bones on my watch."

I roll my eyes and pull the blanket back over my head. "We both know I could miss a few meals. Hey—"

I scowl as the blanket disappears, and Vivian's face appears above me.

"Look, I'm sorry for what I said," she says. She doesn't elaborate, but we both know which insult she's referring to.

No wonder Ellie was so popular. She'd be a meal and a half.

"Are you really?" I ask.

"Yeah. You hadn't even done anything to me, and I lashed out. When I feel threatened or I'm really stressed, I say things that I don't mean. I'm not proud of it. I wish I was someone who instantly started coming up with a plan like Nevada or Ivy or Charlie. Or even someone who started making friends like you. Instead, I turn into the worst version of myself."

"Why?" I ask, curious. "You're gorgeous, and you know it. Why do you need to bring other people down?"

She sighs, pushing my feet over and sitting on the furs. "I dunno. I'm a swimsuit model back home, and over the last few years...I think I've let the pressure get to me. I worked my ass off to look like this, and in a moment, my career was gone." She sighs again, her expression dejected. "I don't think we're getting out of here, Ellie. I think we're stuck. And the only skill I have is posing on the beach."

Wow, who would've thought that someone like Vivian could be so insecure?

"You know, all my life, I've figured that people like you don't have real problems," I admit, and Vivian's mouth drops open before she laughs. "I know, it's a shitty assumption to make. But I've been so wrapped up in my own insecurities that I assumed I was the only one feeling this way."

Vivian sighs. "We've all got something." She gets to her feet. "I'm going to go help in the kitchen. Or the cooking tent or whatever." Her mouth twists wryly. "Things I never thought I'd say. But I figure I may as well make myself useful around here since who knows if we'll end up leaving."

I smile. "With Nevada as determined as she is? You bet your ass that the spaceship will be leaving this planet."

Vivian raises an eyebrow as she gets to her feet. "The spaceship might leave, but will you be on it?"

I sigh, curling back up underneath the furs. "I dunno. I guess that depends on whether Terex still wants me."

Vivian shakes her head like she's disappointed. "Maybe he's waiting for *you* to tell him you want him."

With that, she turns and struts out of the tent.

Ellie

Eventually, Vivian gets tired of me lying around and threatens to douse me in water from the stream if I don't get my ass out of bed.

I move through the camp like I'm sleepwalking, well aware of the whispers following me. By now, it's likely that everyone knows what happened, but I'm too depressed to care about the gossip.

I find Rani playing with the kids in the meadow. She smiles when she sees me, and I blow out a nervous breath. I didn't realize how much I've come to cherish our new friendship.

She murmurs something to the kids, and they laugh but dart away, starting a game with some colored stones.

"Ellie," she says, "how are you?"

I smile, but it quickly falls from my face. By now, she's likely well aware of what's happened with me and Terex.

"I'm not the best," I admit. "But I need to stay busy. I was wondering if I could come back and help with the kids."

Her eyes lighten with sympathy. "Of course you can.

Listen, I'm sorry for what I said about Nevada. I know she's your friend, and I can't imagine what it's been like for you all, taken from your homes with no warning. Truthfully, I'd do whatever it took to get home as well."

"I'm sorry too. I shouldn't have stormed off like that. Of course you're worried about Rakiz. I was just feeling defensive, and I took it out on you."

Rani nods, leaning forward and giving me a hug. I close my eyes, swallowing around the lump in my throat, and pull back, attempting a smile. From the look on Rani's face, my smile has fallen flat.

"Do you need anything?" she asks softly, pushing her hair behind her ear, her golden mating bands catching the light.

"I'm fine, thanks."

"You know, I've known Terex all my life, and I've never seen him as happy as he is when he's with you."

I blink back tears. "I think I ruined it," I say, and she pats me on the shoulder.

"Sometimes, things have to break so they can be built stronger."

I look away, watching the kids play. Moni said something similar a few times when I was in her kradi, and her voice flits through my head. The woman has always slightly freaked me out with the way she seems to stare into my soul.

You can't have healing without pain. Perhaps this is something that you have been slow to learn, hmm?

She's right. All my life, I've let myself be defined by the way my mom and sister labeled me.

I wasn't willing to fight back. To take a stand and deal with the inevitable fallout—and pain—that it would cause.

It wasn't until I saw the way Terex looked at me, the way

he handled me like I was something precious, that I began to question that label.

But I took too long. Now Terex can barely look at me, his gaze flicking away the few times I've seen him. Truthfully, I'm mostly avoiding him, scared I'll find out he's already moving on.

He wouldn't do that to me. I shake the thought off even as I think it. No wonder he's so frustrated with me. At every turn, I expect the giant warrior to betray me. In his mind, I'm constantly questioning his honor.

Terex never once made me feel like I wasn't good enough for him. Never did he imply that I was second best, or that he'd rather be with one of the women who look at him with hungry eyes. Instead, he made it clear that I was the one for him. That I was all he wanted.

And I pushed him away until he gave up.

The thought is so depressing that I want to go back to bed and pull the furs over my head. But I've become part of a community here. The kids rely on me to help them now. I have friends—both human and Braxian. Life is different here, but I fit in more than I could ever have imagined. If Terex never comes back to me, I'll *survive*. I may never be the same, but in this place, I've found an inner strength I never knew I had.

"Ellie?"

"Sorry, Rani. I was having a revelation. Actually, there *is* something you can help me with."

She grins as I tell her about my idea, nodding enthusiastically.

"Of course I can help. But Ellie...are you sure?"

Nope, and the uncertainty in her voice doesn't help me feel any more confident.

"No," I say honestly. "But I have to try."

CHAPTER SIXTEEN

T*erex*

I NARROWLY DODGE A SWORD AIMED FOR MY HEAD, AND A growl leaves my throat. Since the warrior is young, he's using a training sword, but warriors have lost their eyes by becoming distracted during training.

"Good." I nod to Arex, who grins at my praise, lunging forward.

This time, I manage to push my thoughts aside, focusing on the male in front of me. With Rakiz gone, his duties fall to me. There are plenty of other experienced warriors available for training, but after days of dealing with the council's stupid questions and making decisions that directly impact our people, I needed the release of a good training session.

I move to the side, knocking Arex's hand away with my forearm. He almost drops his sword, and I narrow my eyes at him.

"That lunge took you off balance. Remember, Voildi may

be smaller than us, but they're often faster. Two of them could have gutted you in a heartbeat."

His mouth firms, but he nods, stepping back. I partner him with Rovix, a warrior known for his speed in battle. He should be able to teach Arex a few things to make him lighter on his feet.

A small female walks by, close to the training arena, and my heart jumps into my throat. My shoulders slump as I realize she's too tall to be Ellie, and I scowl as I recognize Vivian.

She raises her eyebrow at me but keeps walking, throwing a swing in her step for the gazes of the warriors as she walks by.

I turn, lifting my brows, and training continues.

Ellie has been nowhere to be found for the last few days, although Vivian told me she's staying with her. Each night, I found myself at the entrance to my kradi, ready to take her into my arms and carry her back to my furs.

Last night, I made it close enough to Vivian's kradi to hear the two women's voices. While I couldn't hear what they were saying, the sound of Ellie's soft voice clawed at my guts, and I stood for a long moment, fists clenched as I battled the urge to go to her.

If my tiny female wants me, she will come to me.

This is the mantra I repeat throughout the day. Truthfully, I know I am close to getting on my knees for her. Tonight may be the night that I beg for her to come back to me, desperate for even one more moment with her even if she is to leave me.

I turn from the training arena, cursing. If Ellie does not come to me today...

Perhaps she truly *doesn't* want me.

Ellie

My hands are shaking as I look for Terex. It's now or never. If he still doesn't want me after listening to what I have to say...

I push that thought away. I'll burn that bridge down when I come to it.

I ask around, and Arana tells me where to find Terex. I blow out a breath. Of course he'd be surrounded by people. And it's likely that one or two of them are hoping to replace me in his bed.

I shake my head, blowing out a breath. If I'm going through with this, I've got to let the jealousy go. Before I burned our relationship to the ground, Terex only had eyes for me. He never gave me any indication that he wanted to be with anyone else, never even looked twice at the women who constantly threw themselves at him.

He's loyal, honorable, steadfast. *I'm* the one who let my insecurities take over.

It's now or never.

He's in the common area, near the fire, where he seems to spend most of his time these days. Is he like me—continually searching for distraction? Or would he have enjoyed socializing when I was with him but I prevented it with my jealousy?

I hesitate, palms sweaty while my heart races. Vivian's chatting with one of the other women, pointing to something on her dress, and the woman laughs, smoothing her hand over the fabric.

Vivian locks eyes with me, raising an eyebrow, and I

almost turn and flee, my cheeks heating as the woman she's talking to turns toward me as well.

I blow out a breath, still unable to take a step forward, and she rolls her eyes. Terex moves toward her, asking the other woman a question, and Vivian leans into him, glancing coyly up from beneath her lashes as she murmurs something in a low voice.

Terex smiles at her, and I grind my teeth. I *knew* she couldn't be trusted.

Vivian's ignoring me now, moving closer, and my mouth falls open as she strokes her hand over his shirt, right overtop his scales, laughing up at him.

That's it. I stride forward, blood pounding in my ears. It feels like I'm floating above my body, and I watch as if from a distance as my arms shove her.

"He's mine," I growl. "Back off."

Her mouth widens in shock as she stumbles back. And then she grins at me.

What the hell?

"About damn time you grew a pair. I thought I was going to have to flash him or something before you came over here."

I scowl at her and then close my eyes in mortification as I realize how many people are watching me. For someone who hates attention, I sure create a lot of scenes in this place.

Vivian was just trying to make me woman up and make my move. And my insecurity not only cost me Terex, but it's almost cost me my budding friendship with her as well.

I open my eyes. "I'm sorry," I say.

"Think nothing of it." She smiles at me, and then her eyes flick to Terex, and she moves away, leaving him staring at me.

His eyes aren't cold, but they're not warm either. He's no longer looking at me as if he wants to look at nothing else. Instead, his eyes are wary, as he waits for me to speak.

"Terex—"

"Nothing was happening with her, Ellie," he sighs, glancing away, disappointment stark on his face. He's disappointed in *me,* and it hurts somewhere deep inside.

"I know," I say, and his gaze meets mine. This is it. Now or never. "I realize it's not fair to expect other women not to flirt with you. I can't control that, and I know you don't encourage it. I *know* you want me. At least...you wanted me before I ruined it."

He narrows his eyes, opening his mouth, and I hold up a hand.

"Let me finish," I say. "Please." He nods, but a muscle ticks in his jaw with the effort of staying silent.

"I may not feel like I'm good enough for you. May not truly believe that I'm worthy, but that's something I'll need to work on. You've never given me any reason to be insecure. In fact, you've done the opposite, making me see myself in new ways.

"With you, I'm not awkward and shy. I don't feel like I constantly need to hide away, and I know you'd never do anything to hurt me. I may not understand why you chose me, but if you let me, I'll spend the rest of my life proving that I'm the woman you think I am. I love you, Terex. And I want to stay here on Agron...with you."

I blow out a breath, trembling as I reach into my pocket. I pull out the golden bands, and for the first time, I have the experience of seeing Terex taken completely off guard as his mouth drops open.

Shocked gasps sound, and my face flames as I attempt to ignore the crowd around us. Terex's eyes soften, and I raise my voice, letting the words I've memorized carry so everyone can hear.

"Terex. Will you be my life mate? Will you love me, protect me, always keep me safe, and never stray from my furs? Will you give me children and honor us for the rest of our lives?"

Terex's gaze is fierce, but his voice is hoarse as he holds out his hand.

"I swear," he says, allowing me to tie the bands around his wrists. My hands are shaking so much that I almost can't tie them, but finally, both of the gold mating bands are tied where they'll stay forever.

I open my mouth, unsure what to say next, but Terex growls, pulling me to him with one hand and cupping my cheek with the other.

"My tiny female," he murmurs. "You are so brave." He takes my mouth as the crowd cheers, and I gasp against him, certain I'm dreaming as his hard body finally surrounds mine.

He pulls back, his face flushed, eyes glittering with lust. Then I squeak as he lifts me, cradling me in his arms like a child as he strides toward his kradi. I catch Vivian's laughing gaze, and then Terex ducks his head, and we're finally in his kradi.

Alone.

I nibble nervously at my lip, suddenly unsure what to say, and then Terex pulls me close, taking my lips in a deep kiss,

I sigh against him, still in shock. Somehow, this incredible warrior wants to be mine. Forever.

Terex pulls away, untying my dress until it falls to the floor, and I blink up at him.

His eyes darken as he scans my body and moves close, nuzzling my neck. "What are you thinking?" he murmurs.

"I don't know," I admit. "I think I'm still in shock."

He pulls his head back, gazing down at me. "You have claimed me in front of the tribe," he says. "Now I will claim you in private."

I smile and then shriek in surprise as he lifts me into his arms and strides toward our bed. I shiver as the fur brushes against my naked skin when he places me down, taking my lips once more before he moves back, pulling off his clothes.

I stare avidly at his body, my thighs clenching as he straightens his shoulders under my regard, one corner of his mouth curling up in a sexy grin.

This incredible, loyal, amazing, kind, and ridiculously attractive man is mine. All mine.

And if anyone tries to take him from me, I'll throat punch them.

I blink at that thought, and Terex is suddenly kneeling in front of me.

"What are you thinking?"

"That if anyone tries to take you away, I'll kick their ass."

Terex's shoulders shake as he laughs, his gaze indulgent. "No other females will even attempt such a thing, Ellie." He holds up his wrist, his eyes lit with savage pleasure as we both examine the mating band. "You've claimed me, and everyone in this tribe will respect your claim."

I smile up at him, relieved. Even if someone was to try, I trust Terex, and I know he'd never do anything to hurt me.

"I love you," he tells me seriously, and I blink back tears.

He leans down and kisses the tears that escape my eyes, nuzzling close at my choked sob.

"Thank you for still wanting me...," I whisper, and he leans back with a smile.

"I will always want you."

He takes my lips again, and I close my eyes, breathing in the scent of him.

"Take me," I murmur against his lips, and he growls, leaning me back until I'm surrounded by the soft furs and his hard body.

His breaths are harsh, and his jaw is hard. A groan escapes him when I reach down and wrap my hand around his cock.

He's so big that my fingers don't meet, and I shiver in anticipation. If I hadn't already taken him so many times, I'd be worried, but now all I want is for him to hurry up and get inside me.

Terex nibbles his way down my body, smiling as I shiver and then giggle as he nips at a particularly sensitive spot. Within moments, he's pushing my legs apart, and I arch on the furs as he licks along my slit before sucking on my clit as I bury my hands in his hair.

"God, Terex..."

He pushes two fingers inside me, thrusting them as he plays with my clit, and the world disappears, his talented mouth and fingers the only things that exist.

"Aaah," I groan as my body blasts apart, and I shudder, engulfed by pleasure.

Terex moves up my body, pausing to place kisses along my collarbone. "I love you," he says again. He intertwines his fingers with mine, and his large cock slides into me, feeling so incredibly *right* that I groan as my eyes flutter shut.

"Look at me," he says, and I meet his violet gaze, trembling at the wealth of emotion he lets me see.

He pulls out and thrusts again, pushing our hands above my head, cradling me beneath him. I feel so small and delicate...protected, with his huge body surrounding me.

I raise my hips, wrapping my legs around him and gasping as he grinds against my clit on his next thrust. He does it again, driving into me faster until everything but him disappears, and I'm groaning out his name, clamping my legs around him as I tremble on the edge.

"Oh, God..."

Pleasure rips through me, and I see stars as I'm consumed by my orgasm. Terex growls, shaking against me as he empties within me, still thrusting until he collapses, pressing against me for a single moment before he twists, dragging me on top of him while we both recover, panting.

"Wow," I say. I never knew sex could be like this. Never knew it could feel like handing your soul over to someone but getting theirs in return.

"Wow is right." Terex brings my hand to his lips, pressing kisses against my fingers, and I raise my head, meeting his gaze.

I'll never get enough of him—this man who forced me to be the woman he knew I could be. He made me realize I'm worthy of love, made me *fight* for what I needed. Him.

I nuzzle his chest, stroking one hand along the glimmering scales that will never cease to fascinate me.

"This time," I say, as I straddle his huge body, "I get to be on top."

EPILOGUE

E*llie*

"Miss Ellie, Miss Ellie, come look!"

I turn, smiling down at some of the kids. I'm not sure who told them to call me Miss Ellie, but my guess is it was Vivian. Since I laid down the law regarding my giant warrior, both of us have come to an uneasy truce.

Like it or not, we're the only humans here. We only have each other.

Nevada is still gone, and no one has heard from Rakiz. Granted, it's only been a week or so, but Terex's face is often hard, his gaze worried when he returns to our kradi. When he sees me, his eyes lighten to the violet color that tells me he's thinking about "tumbling" me.

A shard of worry stabs me in the gut even as I follow the kids to where something is lying in the grass. The smell hits me before I can get any closer.

"Ew, you guys, get away from there." I gag as one of the older boys pokes it with a stick.

Whatever it is, it's dead, and a cold sweat breaks out on my neck as the boy flips over the body with his stick.

"Oooh," one of the girls says as the entrails slither out, and that's it for me.

I lean over, puking in the grass, and *that's* when the kids choose to be disgusted.

"*Gross*, Miss Ellie's sick!"

Vomiting is never fun, but it's even worse in public and surrounded by curious eyes.

"I can see what you had for breakfast," one of the boys laughs, and I glare at him even as I lean over and retch again.

"What are you do—Ellie, are you okay?"

I gasp, wiping my mouth with the back of my hand. "I will be if these little demons will leave me alone."

The kids laugh as I meet Rani's concerned gaze.

She leads me away from the stench and guides me onto a small seat that someone has carved into a fallen log.

I breathe through my mouth, but I feel like the world is dancing around me as the sweat begins to cool on the back of my neck.

"Are you sick, Ellie?"

I put my head down between my legs, and some of the nausea recedes. "I mean, it's a dead animal," I mutter. "I'm not really the outdoors type, if you hadn't noticed. But I still feel a bit off. Maybe I've got some kind of virus or something."

"I'll go find Terex."

"No, don't bother him. He's so busy right now with Rakiz gone. I'm fine, I just need to go lie down."

I raise my head and attempt to smile at Rani, but I can tell she's not buying it.

"Ellie," she murmurs softly, leaning close. "Is there a possibility that you could be...pregnant?"

I almost clasp my hand over the translator in my ear as I stare at her, automatically shaking my head.

"No, I'm on the..." I trail off, stunned. I'm not on the pill. My contraceptive is currently sitting in my makeup bag in my mother's bathroom. Actually, it's more likely to have been collected as evidence when I disappeared.

I had some breakthrough bleeding when I first arrived, but everything had been so crazy that I haven't even thought about the consequences of jumping my warrior every chance I get.

Pregnant.

I mean, it's possible.

"Do you know how long we've been here for, Rani?"

She furrows her brow, and then her eyes widen. "Actually, I remember you arrived on my mother's birthday. We were walking back from her kradi, and we stopped to watch when you arrived with Terex and the other warriors."

"How long ago was that?"

"One moon cycle."

Okay, good talk.

I blow out a breath, frustrated that I still haven't learned the basics about this planet. I have a lot of integrating to do if I could potentially be raising a rug rat. The thought makes my stomach clench nervously, and I put my head back between my legs.

"How many days in a moon cycle?"

"Forty-five days."

Yup, I've definitely missed my period.

"Ellie?"

I look up as Terex appears, face stark with concern. One of the kids must have found him. While I didn't want him disturbed, I'm grateful when he takes me into his arms.

Rani smiles at me and leads the kids away to give us privacy.

"Tell me what is wrong, my Ellie."

My heart flips when he calls me that, and I raise my hand to his cheek. "I'm fine, really. I just got a little sick. But, the thing is…" I trail off, suddenly unsure. I'm secure in my relationship with Terex, but we've known each other for less than two months. Sure, we lived together immediately and went through life-and-death experiences that brought us much closer together. But what if he's not ready to be a dad?

I nibble on my lip, and Terex swings me into his arms, sitting back down with me on his lap.

He nuzzles my cheek. "You can tell me anything, tiny female. You know that."

"I know." I take a deep breath, and the words leave me in a rush. "I'm pretty sure I'm pregnant."

His face is blank for a moment, and then his eyes light up, shining bright, and his white teeth flash as he grins like I've handed him the moon. "A child?"

I nod, biting my lip, and his gaze drops to my stomach, his huge hand resting on my lower abdomen. I choke out a laugh that's more like a sob.

"So you're happy?"

"Happy? Happiness doesn't come close to what I feel in this moment. The best day of my life was the day I found you in that forest. I promise I will spend the rest of my life making sure you never regret your decision to stay with me."

My eyes fill with tears, and Terex brushes them off my cheeks.

Terex grins down at me. "Now that I have claimed you in

every way, will you finally complete the mating ceremony with me?"

I frown at him. I've been putting off the ceremony—not because I don't want to be his mate but because Nevada's not here. I know Terex misses Rakiz too. But if I'm knocked up...

It's not that I'm religious or that I feel a woman should *have* to be married—or mated—before she has a baby. But if I'm honest, the thought of waiting even one more day...

"I know Nevada will forgive *me*," I say. "But won't Rakiz be mad at you?"

Terex throws his head back, laughing in the way that never fails to make my heart beat a little faster.

"Rakiz is a warrior who has left his tribe to hunt for a human female. He'll understand my need to tie those mating bands on your wrists before anyone else thinks to do the same."

I laugh at the idea that giant warriors are lining up to claim me, but Terex's face is serious, so who am I to argue if he wants to believe I'm that incredible? I'm no dummy.

At least, not anymore.

"Fine," I laugh as he stands with me still in his arms, careful not to jostle me. "But if I puke on you when I'm thrown over the fire...it's on you."

His eyes laugh down at me as he turns to walk toward our kradi, and I grin back at him.

Somehow, getting abducted by aliens led to everything I've secretly always wanted but never dreamed I could have. Agron may not be for everyone, but with my warrior's arms wrapped around me, I wouldn't be anywhere else.

The End

I hope you enjoyed Taken by the Alien Warrior! If you did, please consider leaving a review— these help indie authors to attract new readers.

Want more of Ellie and Terex? Sign up for my newsletter to receive a *free* **bonus** **chapter** along with regular updates about new books and freebies.

Rakiz and Nevada's story is next. Keep reading for a sneak peek!

CLAIMED BY THE ALIEN WARRIOR

N*evada*

"MOVE THAT BACK LEG."

I adjust, nodding as I switch to a slightly more comfortable fighting stance.

The only difference between fighting on Agron and fighting on Earth?

The sword in my hand.

That hand trembles, and I scowl. Turns out my wrists are nowhere near as strong as they should be if I'm planning to wield a sword on this planet.

The Braxians are bigger than me, stronger than me, tougher than me, and usually faster than me.

The good news? I'm not planning to fight Braxians.

I'm going after the Voildi. They're still bigger than us humans, but if I'm smart, I might at least have a chance.

"Okay," Asroz says. "What are your three rules?"

"Strike first, think smart, and fight dirty."

He nods. For whatever reason, Asroz has decided to train me. Most of the warriors here were amused and then appalled when I started learning how to fight with a sword. I think Asroz is also amused, but in his words, if I'm determined to learn, he may as well prevent me from waving my sword around like an asshole.

Okay, those weren't his exact words.

I can barely lift the giant swords that these warriors carry. So Asroz kindly gave me a training sword. Yesterday, he finally sharpened it, and in theory, I should be ready to go.

Yeah, right.

We're practicing with wooden swords for now, which is good 'cause otherwise I'd probably have lost more than one limb already.

"Why will you strike first?" Asroz asks.

"Because I need the element of surprise. No one will expect a woman to be any good with a sword. And once they decide to cut me down, I don't have the muscle strength to absorb the force of an overhead blow."

"Think smart?"

"Only attack if necessary. Plan, lay traps, and use my surroundings."

"Good. And why will you fight dirty?"

I grin. Truthfully, I don't know how to fight any other way.

"I've got hand-to-hand combat experience—something many creatures here don't have. They're used to relying on their swords. A hit to the nuts hurts the same whether you're human or Voildi."

"Good."

I've been surprised by how seriously Asroz is taking this training. Most people assume he's just indulging me, but he's not an idiot. He knows I'm planning to go after our friends. And he's hoping to give me the best possible chance of coming out alive.

"Time for your drills."

I nod, ready. Unlike one would probably expect, most of my drills don't involve using my sword at all. Instead, they're all about speed. On this planet, the fact that I'm light on my feet is about all I've got going for me.

Unlike what I expected after a lifetime of watching Hollywood movies, blocking a sword is my last line of defense. Asroz has taught me some fancy footwork, and the goal is that I simply won't be there when a sword is aimed at my head.

I raise my sword, and Asroz attacks. I've got a feeling he's still nowhere near to using his full speed, but I'm definitely getting faster.

His strikes come one after the other, and I dodge, weave, and pivot, gradually moving backward until I can duck under his arm.

My sword comes up, and I slide it along his ribs. He stops and grins at me, pleased.

"Point," he says. "But that should have been a thrust. I was off-balance, and my heart was right there."

I blow out a breath. I'm a marine. I've seen combat. I've killed before. But the idea of sliding a sword into someone's heart doesn't come naturally.

"This needs to be instinct," Asroz says, and I nod. Just like when fighting a guy who outweighs me on Earth, I have to be brutal. Flesh wounds are just going to piss them off.

And since the Voildi are usually in packs, I don't have time to fuck around.

Sweat is dripping in my eyes by the time we're finished, and I turn, not at all surprised to find an audience. Men outnumber women on this planet by ten to one, and the women? They wear dresses.

If I were running in a floor-length dress, I'd be guaranteed to faceplant.

The people here aren't shy about staring, and while I used to make a point of meeting each of their gazes, now I just tend to ignore them.

The reason for the scandalized looks currently coming my way? The leather pants I'm wearing. Honestly, I'm not sure what offends the locals more—the sword in my hand, my filthy mouth, or the pair of Brexian pants I stole. Luckily, the seamstress seemed to find my request hilarious, and she's currently working on another pair for me, along with some shirts.

I'd kill for a bath right about now. Sure, I'd rather shower, but you take what you can get in this place. I wipe sweat off my forehead with the back of my hand, once again ignoring the eyes on me as I make my way to the mishua pen.

No point getting clean when I'm about to be working with the mishua.

This is my "punishment."

A few days ago, I had a minor freak-out. I decided I couldn't take the waiting around anymore and attempted to sneak out of the camp.

Truthfully, I'm glad I was caught. No, I didn't enjoy the chewing out I was given by Rakiz, the tribe king, but leaving unprepared is a bad idea. I was planning to go on foot but quickly realized my mistake: I need to move faster.

I eye the mishua as I get closer. They're not the most attractive beasts, but they can cover more ground in a few hours than I can in an entire day of walking. They're intelligent, dangerous, and moody as fuck.

But you know what? So am I.

Mishua don't tolerate females riding them. Personally, I wonder if it's a chicken-and-egg situation. Maybe they're just not used to females, since the women around here wouldn't dream of riding alone.

Rakiz's voice runs through my head as I open the pen and stride inside.

"You want to dress like a male and fight like a male? Fine. You can also work like a male. You will work with the mishua until I believe you have learned your lesson."

I promised him he'd regret that decision. And it turns out that working with the mishua is good for me in two ways. First, it's helping to strengthen my forearms and wrists, which is exactly what I need to wield a sword. But more importantly, I have the perfect opportunity to convince a mishua to let me sit on its back.

"Hi, girls," I say as I stride through the pen. The mishua have gotten used to me already and pay me little attention, although a few of them snort at me as I get close.

When the Brexians saved us from the Voildi, I took one look at their mishua and dubbed them *dino-horses.* They're lizard-looking dark-green creatures with mouthfuls of sharp fangs, horns covering their snouts, and huge heads. Oh, and weirdly, the bottoms of their legs are covered in thick fur.

The mishua have intimidating red eyes and bad attitudes. They're fierce in battle and can travel long distances without needing a break.

I'm pretty sure they can't understand English, but I've been talking to them anyway, hoping they'll get used to the sound of my voice.

"I'm getting better with the sword," I tell one of them, and she stares at me for a moment, red eyes glinting, before she turns her back on me.

Yeah, it's tough going. But no worse than the popular girls in high school.

Weirdly, the mishua that pays me the most attention happens to be Rakiz's preferred mount. She's bigger than the rest, and her eyes hold an intelligence that freaks me out ever so slightly.

"Hey, Racia. Wow, bet you're bored in here, huh?"

She stares at me as I get closer, snorting at me in warning, and I stop in my tracks.

"Wow, someone's pissy today. Probably cause you haven't been out for a while. When *was* the last time you went out anyway?" I tut, shaking my head as if saddened. "It's such a shame the king is always hanging around at camp. You must get so bored."

On the off chance that the mishua can understand me, I want to sow the seeds that will one day make her tolerate me on her back.

I turn and mosey on over to the sleeping area, where I've stowed the huge shovel I was given. My task? Mucking out the mishua pen.

The tribe was astounded to hear about my punishment, and I've even caught regret in Rakiz's eyes once or twice. But he'll never go back on his word, and he may think this is the worst task I've ever done, but it's not even close.

My uncle had horses when I was a kid, and he always made me muck out the stables in exchange for a ride. Poop doesn't bother me. Although, these huge creatures produce more of it than any animal I've ever seen.

I lean over, ignoring the eyes on me as I get to work. The people here like to stare. I get it—I'm different. But it's hard to plan my escape when I'm being watched like a hawk.

The good news? There are fewer people leaning against

the fence than there were yesterday. Hopefully these people will get bored soon too and leave me alone.

While I can block out most of the attention, one hard gaze is more difficult to ignore. I look up as Rakiz walks past, his council trailing in his steps, and I sneer at him as he nods at me.

Rakiz may be the tribe king, but as I've told him before, that doesn't mean he's *my* king.

His eyes lighten with amusement, and I turn away. For whatever reason, out of all the huge warriors here, Rakiz is the one that makes my thighs clench.

I just don't get it.

He's bossy and overbearing and refuses to take me seriously. Due to the shortage of females on this planet, the males here seem to think that females should be coddled and protected.

When I tried to explain that I was more than capable of helping to look for our friends, Rakiz did everything but pat me on the head.

And then he had the gall to be furious when I decided to go on my own.

Shoveling shit gives me a lot of time to myself. Unfortunately, that means I have a lot of hours to think about my life on Earth.

I can't stand the idea that everyone will think I went AWOL. I was on leave, visiting my friend Kat, when I went for a walk to get some air.

That's the last thing I remember.

It was late at night, and I was wearing shorts and a tank top—more than most of the other women, the majority of whom were taken from their beds. I had my car keys and phone, and I hope to God someone found them deserted somewhere and everyone knows I was taken and that I didn't just leave.

I'd never go AWOL on purpose.

I can't think about that now. My focus has to be on finding the other women so we can get the hell off this planet.

Rakiz

I almost laugh as Nevada glowers at me. The human female is currently cleaning out the mishua pen, yet she still looks as arrogant as ever.

Something about this female calls to me—even though every time I spend more than a few moments in her presence, I feel the urge to shake some sense into her.

My punishment has not been well received by my tribe. Surprisingly, it is the females who have supported it the most. My warriors, however, are mostly shocked that I would give a female such physical work.

My reasoning was that Nevada would be so tired at the end of each day that she would no longer have the energy to make the kinds of plans that will get her killed.

Unfortunately, the hellion simply began training earlier with Asroz, and I strongly suspect she considers her work in the mishua pen to be an extension of her workout.

I almost groan as Nevada bends over, her well-toned ass flexing in her pants. Numerous females have demanded that I take those pants away, but watching Nevada stalk through the camp with leather hugging her long legs is one of the few pleasures I have. I'd be an idiot to take them from her.

Plus, she would likely attempt to castrate me.

I sigh as my councilors start again.

"Really, your majesty, I just think—"

"Enough." I hold up a hand, wishing for nothing more than some peace and quiet. Truthfully, I'd rather be working in the mishua pen with Nevada than listening to the councilors' complaints.

"You have more than enough time to bring these concerns to me during our meetings. Why must you follow me around camp each day like children following their mother?"

Silence surrounds me, and I sigh. I am growing short-tempered. The fact that a single female is responsible for my bad mood is not lost on me.

After her escape attempt, I ordered Nevada to sleep in my tashiv, which is the most guarded place in the camp. She refused until I threatened to tie her to me while I slept. Now she creeps into her furs on the other side of the room each night once she believes I am already asleep. Then she creeps back out before the sun rises each morning.

This morning, I didn't even wake when she left.

My guards have been ordered to stop her if she attempts to leave again at night. Unfortunately, I don't trust the hellion's current good behavior at all.

I scowl as the councilor starts up again and move back toward my tashiv. I tune him out as I walk, nodding to my warriors as they head toward the training arena.

How can I convince the stubborn female that to leave this camp would be suicide? She believes that I'm not working to find her friends when my every decision is based on freeing up more of my warriors to hunt for the other females.

It still stuns me that such small females are here on our planet. If my men hadn't seen their spaceship with their own eyes, I would struggle to believe that it exists. Unfortunately, as soon as the females landed, a pack of Voildi discovered the ship and convinced the females that they were saving them. The Voildi were leading them to certain death when Terex—the leader of my warriors—located them.

Now, four of the females are still missing—three of them likely still in the hands of the Voildi and one taken by Dragix, our great ancestor.

Our tribe is down to three human females, with the one known as Alexis choosing to exchange her freedom for information about the lost female. She has chosen to stay with Dexar, a warrior who can only sometimes be trusted.

My body tenses at the thought. When Asroz told me that one of the females had stayed...

I marched to my mishua, ready to drag Nevada back by her hair if I had to. It was a possessive, irrational reaction, and I still don't understand it.

Neither do I understand the way I buried my hand in the stubborn female's lush hair and took her mouth when I realized she had returned.

To me.